LOST GOLD

Center Point
Large Print

**This Large Print Book carries the
Seal of Approval of N.A.V.H.**

LOST GOLD

A Western Duo

Todhunter Ballard

CENTER POINT LARGE PRINT
THORNDIKE, MAINE

This Center Point Large Print edition
is published in the year 2015 in conjunction with
Golden West Literary Agency.

The text of this Large Print edition is unabridged.
In other aspects, this book may vary
from the original edition.
Printed in the United States of America on permanent paper.
Set in 16-point Times New Roman type.

ISBN: 978-1-62899-445-2 (hardcover)
ISBN: 978-1-62899-450-6 (paperback)

Library of Congress Cataloging-in-Publication Data

Ballard, Todhunter, 1903–1980.
[Novels. Selections]
Lost gold : a western duo / Todhunter Ballard. — Center Point Large Print edition.
pages ; cm
Summary: "Two western stories centered around two young women whose lives are thrown into turmoil because of the men around them and the lure of gold"—Provided by publisher.
ISBN 978-1-62899-445-2 (hardcover : alk. paper)
ISBN 978-1-62899-450-6 (pbk. : alk. paper)
1. Large type books.
   I. Ballard, Todhunter, 1903–1980. Dragon was a lady.
   II. Ballard, Todhunter, 1903–1980. Lost gold. III. Title.
PS3503.A5575A6 2015
813´.52—dc23
                                                        2014041790

TABLE OF CONTENTS

The Dragon Was a Lady

I

Stepping from the Beatty stage into the coarse dust of Goat Springs' raw main street, Faith Thorndyke had no idea that within six weeks she would promise herself to Lazarus Howe, who had been her father's attorney. She had never met the man, and had only a single letter from him, an eloquent and sympathetic report of her father's death, an assurance that he would continue to handle the affairs of the mine and the town as he had for old Gus.

Grimy and worn out from the long drive, she stood in the hot desert sun and had her first look at the ugly mining town where her father had been king, and, in the loneliness of that moment, marriage was the farthest thing from her mind.

She was a small slip of a girl with hair the color of warm taffy and big gray eyes that looked serious, but could darken until they were almost black when she was aroused.

She had not seen her father since her fifth birthday, but his letters had come regularly, their postmarks forming a rough map of the Western world until he had finally written that he had struck it rich on the eastern edge of Death Valley, that he had incorporated the mine for 5,000,000 shares, was building a town, and intended to build the biggest

9

house in the world at the head of Mantel Gulch.

From his description she had formed an exciting picture of Goat Springs, and her first view of the place filled her with shocked disappointment. Only the bank and the hotel, with its stock exchange annex, were substantially built. The rest of the straggling structures were unpainted timber or canvas tents stretched over wooden frames.

The deep dust burned through her shoes, and the overhead sun spread a blanket of hot air almost too thick to breathe. Faith felt a small lump of wretchedness forming in her throat, standing alone and uncertain on the board sidewalk beside the stage. She looked around a little hopelessly. There were loafers in the shade of the wooden awning before Gettler's store, but they made no move to come forward and the rest of the street was silent and deserted in the heat. Then she turned and her eyes met those of the biggest man she had ever seen.

He was across the street, his wide shoulders braced against the wooden frame of a tent and above his head was a crudely lettered sign that read:

GOAT SPRINGS NEWS—JOB PRINTING
MARCUS GORMAN, EDITOR AND OWNER

The big man's hair was black and uncut and curled down over the open collar of his tan shirt.

His sleeves were rolled, showing his forearms, big but not muscle twisted. His hat was stiff-brimmed, but came up to a conical peak like a Mexican sombrero, weather-stained and worn.

For a moment neither moved as their eyes locked, then his boots cracked in the gravelly dust and he crossed to the stage, caught the end of her trunk, and hefted it.

"You'll hurt yourself," she warned. "It's heavy."

He gave her a slow, steady look, then, still without speaking, he lifted the trunk from the boot and swung it easily to the sidewalk at her feet.

Something in the gesture angered Faith. "A great strong man," she told him cuttingly, "anxious to show off. You're lucky if you didn't hurt your back."

A wry smile touched his lips, then he stepped away, but, as he started back across the street, a carriage swirled up behind the stage and a man dropped to the ground, his thin, nervous face flushed with anger.

"Keep away from her, Gorman, you and your lies."

Gorman's turning motion was almost a blur. The smaller man's hand had snaked under his dark, long-skirted coat, but he wasn't fast enough, for the big man caught his wrist and twisted until a gun dropped heavily to the ground between them. Gorman pushed then, and the newcomer staggered back a step, and in that moment the big man stooped, caught up the gun, and, with a little mocking bow that included the girl, he swung away, plodding unconcernedly toward the tent to disappear without looking back through the curtained door of the print shop.

Faith Thorndyke stared after him with uncomprehending eyes. The action in the street had been too fast for her to follow, too abrupt for her to understand.

The new arrival pulled himself together and managed a smile. "You're Faith Thorndyke," he said. "I'm Lazarus Howe. I'm sorry your reception was so trying and that I wasn't here when the stage arrived."

Faith found swift relief in Howe's presence. He helped her into the carriage and turned it, driving back up the gulch toward her father's big house.

"What was the quarrel all about?" Faith asked.

Howe's lips twisted in a bitter smile. "Don't worry about Gorman," he told her. "The man is nothing but a tough. The country is filled with people like him, but they won't bother you if you stay away from the business section. As for the fight, we have an old misunderstanding."

"But he took your gun."

"My own fault." Howe's bitterness grew. "I'm not a gunman and I shouldn't try and fight Gorman on his own ground. It's a mistake I'll try not to make again. This is a rough camp, my dear. There are several thousand miners, toughs, saloonkeepers, gamblers, and the like. I want your promise that you won't go into town alone. As long as your father lived, he kept things well in hand, but, since his death, things haven't been as well controlled."

Faith wasn't exactly satisfied, but there were so many things to learn, so much that was new and startling. The house proved very disconcerting. It wasn't the largest in the world, but it certainly was bigger than any other in Goat Springs. The furnishings took her breath away. They were the best available in San Francisco and had cost a fortune. So had the house. The workmanship was fine. The materials the best; even the doorknobs were of solid silver.

The housekeeper was as disconcerting as the house. Faith found that she was a little afraid of Myra Perkins. The woman was tall and thin and close-mouthed. Her husband had been killed in the mine, and she seldom spoke unless she was spoken to.

She was little company, and for Faith days were long and hot and bleak, but the evenings were wonderful. It turned cool then, and the desert hills changed color minute by minute until the rich darkness blanketed the raw land, softening the bare outline of the rocks and laying a soothing hand over the tortured desert. And with evening Lazarus came, sometimes alone, sometimes with a party of friends. He was a gay companion; he knew how to make her laugh.

She was not surprised when he proposed. She knew a slight sense of being rushed, but, after all, this was a new land where people did not waste time. It gave an excited importance to living that she mistook for love.

Once she had agreed, Lazarus wasted no time. They sat in the big room and made their hurried plans. They would be married the following week. With this in mind they summoned some friends to help prepare the guest list.

Everyone was pleased and eager to make this a royal event. Goat Springs did not offer many social occasions. They planned the decorations for the house, and Mrs. Ames, the mayor's wife, ensconced herself at the table and wrote down the names of the prospective guests. For the first time Faith Thorndyke saw the shadings of a mining camp's society as the eligibility of each candidate was exhaustively discussed.

There were forty who finally qualified—mining company officials and their wives, brokers from the local stock exchange, the president of the bank, and a few of the leading merchants for democracy's sake. It was an impressive list, but Faith read it with the feeling that something important was lacking. "Shouldn't we have someone from the newspaper? I'd like to have the wedding written up so I can send the account to my friends in the East."

Sudden silence blanketed the big room until

Lazarus said hurriedly: "There isn't any paper in Goat Springs, dear."

Faith Thorndyke was surprised. "But surely I saw the office the day I arrived. Don't you remember that man named Gorman you quarreled with? His name was over the door."

Lazarus Howe would as soon have invited a rattlesnake to his wedding as to ask Mark Gorman. If there was one man in Goat Springs he did not want his future wife to talk to, it was Gorman.

"I told you he was tough," Howe said curtly. "When I get over to Rhyolite, I'll give the story to the *Review*. No self-respecting person ever reads the Goat Springs *News*."

Mrs. Ames came to Lazarus's aid. "And you wouldn't want Mark Gorman in your house." She came over and put a large arm around Faith's shoulders. "You poor dear, if it wasn't for Mark Gorman, old Gus Thorndyke would probably still be alive today and you wouldn't be an orphan."

Faith was horrified. "You mean this Gorman killed my father?"

The mayor's wife was thoroughly enjoying herself. "Well, he didn't shoot him, but he killed him nonetheless. Ever since Gorman got that press, he's been taking pot shots at old Gus and the mine and Lazarus and all of us. Finally he ran a front page editorial in which he called your father a pirate and Captain Kidd . . . and a lot of other names. It made Gus so mad that he started up those stairs." She pointed to the open staircase with its hand-carved balustrade. "He was going to get his gun and go down and personally run Gorman out of town. But halfway up, he had his heart attack. He fell backward and broke his neck."

The silence in the big room was strained. Lazarus's face was dead white. He signaled to the mayor who hustled his wife from the room. The other guests left hastily and Lazarus came back alone.

"I'm terribly sorry," he said in his soft voice. "I tried to stop her. There was no need for you to hear the details of your father's death."

"You should have told me." Faith's voice was low and troubled.

"What good would it have done?" The lawyer was patient. "It just makes you feel worse. Your father had quite a temper, and he'd taken a number of things from Gorman. That editorial was the last straw. He'd tried a dozen times to buy the lying paper, but Gorman is bull-headed. He won't listen to anyone."

She said slowly, not looking at him: "This . . . this Gorman, if he writes lies all the time, I'm surprised that someone hasn't stopped him before this."

"Well . . ."—Lazarus's fingers went to his small mustache, twisting it nervously—"you saw him on that morning you arrived. He's very big, and

16

he's very quick with a gun, and a lot of people in this town fear him. I guess they have a right to. He killed a man over in Goldfield."

She stared, horrified. "Killed a man in Goldfield! You mean he's a murderer? But why hasn't he been arrested and tried. I'd think that . . ."

Lazarus had to smile in sprite of his anger. "There isn't much law out this way. . . ."

"Someone should stop him. Someone should do something. . . ."

"I'm going to take care of Mister Gorman, but don't worry your pretty head about it. You and I have something much more important to think of at the moment. We have to get married." He leaned forward and kissed her. "Get everything ready for the wedding, darling."

Long after he had driven away, she stood on the wide porch looking out across the town below. She could hear the noise from the lower gulch faintly, and beyond, at the drop off of the hill, she could see the lights of the mine head frame.

This is my world, she thought. *It's my town, my mine. I've got to get used to living out here. I've got to begin to understand the country and the people.*

She was still thinking of this during the week that followed, while she and Myra Perkins cleaned and baked and planned the routine for the volunteer helpers who would be there on her wedding day.

II

It gave her quite a start to wake up one morning and realize this was the day. For a few moments she wasn't sure she was glad about it, but then Myra was calling from the stairs, reminding her of all that was still to be done, and she was caught up in the bustle of preparations.

"We'll have forty guests," Faith said. She was as excited as a little girl. "We'll make place cards!" She produced the list. "I hope they all come because Lazarus has already taken the story over to the Rhyolite *Review*."

The housekeeper turned to look at her, a gaunt woman, the flesh on her neck and arms seemingly dried on the bone structure beneath. At first she'd expected to resent Gus Thorndyke's daughter, but to her surprise she had come to like and feel a little sorry for the girl. Faith was so alone, so obviously inexperienced, so puzzled by her new surroundings, yet she never complained.

Myra liked that. She even permitted herself a wintry smile as she said: "I'll bet Mark Gorman's *News* beats the *Review* on the story for all of Lazarus's fancy footwork. It ain't often that Mark gets the chance to whittle his pen on the antics of Goat Springs' society."

Faith looked up in surprise. "But how can he get

the story? He isn't invited, and, after what Missus Ames said, he certainly isn't going to be."

Myra Perkins hooted. "Genevieve Ames. Her and her airs. I remember when she was washing dishes in a Tonopah restaurant. Why, her and the rest of that bunch she runs with ain't fit to wipe the dirt from Mark Gorman's boots."

Faith had stopped work. She said a little breathlessly: "You know him then?"

"Know him? I practically raised him, the young hellion. His daddy taught school at Minton and done assaying on the side. Everybody in the country knows Mark and mostly they like him, at least the ones that have nothing to hide."

"But he caused my father's death."

The older woman's hard face softened a little. "I don't go around speaking of the dead, honey, but your daddy's own temper was what give him the attack. A man like your father is bound to have differences with newspapers, now and then."

Faith was adamant. "And Gorman murdered a man in Goldfield."

Myra was unmoved. "Shucks, honey, that tramp he shot in Goldfield sure deserved killing. Mark just happened to come along when the man was on the prod. The jury wasn't out three minutes. They wouldn't even have tried him, only Mark insisted. He's kind of funny that way, always for law and order and such. Why, he ain't no gunman, he's just a poor prospector."

Faith was nonplussed. "But I thought he owned the *News*."

The housekeeper laughed. "Honey, he won that printing press in a poker game. He didn't want it. He tried all over camp to sell it or give it away, but no one wanted it, so he just naturally started a paper. He sure had a time at first. Mark never did learn to spell very well. It was a struggle, I can promise you."

By this time Faith was thoroughly confused. "So that's it. He's a gambler."

Myra was indignant. "He's not a gambler. A real gambler never works, and Mark Gorman works like hell. He's like most of the boys . . . he plays cards for fun, and he isn't bad. I recall when he first started the *News*. I met him on the street, and he stopped to tell me his trouble. Spelling was one of them, so I told him . . . 'Don't let spelling throw you, boy. Your father couldn't spell, either, and he was the best damn' teacher this country ever saw. What's spelling?' " She paused and dusted the flour from her fingers. " 'They've got books with all the words spelled right in them. You go right ahead with that paper and make a good job of it.' That's what he done, too. He couldn't have done better if he'd been able to spell twice as good. He sure is carving his initials on Goat Springs, and some of us like it."

She was interrupted by a knock at the rear door, and the Indian boy, who cared for the horses, brought in a package and dumped it at Faith's feet and went out without a word.

The package was light and Faith tore open a corner exposing billowy white tulle. "Oh Myra, it's my wedding dress!" Her voice got a little quivery with freshened excitement. "Missus Creig sent it up. It was hers, and there wasn't time for a new one. I hope it fits."

The housekeeper's face softened. "There now, honey. It'll fit. Esther Creig wasn't the same shape in those days as she is now. You run along and try it on. I'll be up as soon as I get the bread out of the oven."

In a rush of happiness Faith leaned forward and kissed her, then pirouetted out of the kitchen and danced up the grand staircase.

Behind her Myra Perkins wiped her nose briskly on the corner of her checkered apron and turned, muttering, toward the stove.

In her own room Faith tore off the wrappings and held the dress up before her, looking into the mirror. It was beautiful. She knew she was going to cry. This was the happiest day of her life. She wriggled quickly out of her gingham house dress and dropped the frothy gown down over her taffy hair. The fit was good. The bodice could have been made especially for her, although the cascading ruffles of the skirt were a trifle too long. She pivoted, admiring herself in the long glass, and then reached for the veil, still caught in the newspaper wrappings. She freed it and pinned the net into her curls, and then stopped suddenly. The crumpled paper spread out at her feet was a copy of the Goat Springs *News* and her name was in the headline.

MORE TROUBLE FOR THE CAMP
Faith Thorndyke to Marry

Slowly she stooped to pick up the paper. After the weeklies she had known in the East, it was not impressive—a single sheet, folded in the middle to make four pages. The heading letters were crooked and irregular as if they had been cut from a pine block with the help of a jackknife.

GOAT SPRING NEWS
All The News That's Fit To Print
And Some That Ain't
Marcus Gorman, Editor

Below, the whole front page was devoted to the wedding story. Apparently someone had tipped off Gorman of the doings at the big house, for he wrote:

As we go to press, the news comes over our private grapevine that the queen is taking a consort. Yep, you guessed it, she's marrying up with Lazarus Howe, and I guess we couldn't have expected no more, she being Gus's daughter, but it does seem a miscarriage of all fired pretty meterial.

Faith Thorndyke wears her old man's boots and uses them to stomp with. Goat Springs hoped that when the old highbinder, Gus Thorndyke, turned in his chips that there might be a new deal. We heard he had a pretty daughter, although we couldn't figure how the old polecat could have sired anything that would be fit to look at in the light of day. We figured that no woman would put up with the gang of cut-throats that Gus had around him. Again we're wrong. She's marrying the worst of them and he'll keep on operating high, wide, and handsome, stealing everything he can lay his hands on.

Since she owns the mine, the bank, and the town, you might think this sweet little girl could see that the poor miners, who she only pays $3 a day, wouldn't be bamboozled into giving it back for her worthless stock. But no, her appatyte for money is bigger than her father's ever was. She can't possibly use it all herself, so we figure she keeps a dragon hidden up in her castle which costs her a lot to feed. If we're wrong, if there ain't no dragon, we hereby apologise and take off our hat to the money grabbenest woman we ever heard about.

Faith Thorndyke couldn't believe her eyes. She read the smudged page twice, then she hurled the paper across the room, using a word she had heard from Myra Perkins.

"The damned hypocrite!" she yelled. "I'll show him his dragon, all right. I'll show it to him right now. If the rest of them are afraid to run him out of town, I'm not." She crossed to the window, opened it, and yelled down to the Indian boy to harness the horses to the carriage. She raced down the stairs, the wedding veil flowing like a pennant behind her.

Myra Perkins saw her from the window and thought that Faith must have lost her mind. The Indian boy, holding the horses beside the hitching block, had to jump for his life, for Faith landed in the carriage, entirely forgetting that she still wore the wedding dress, seized the reins, and started off down the rocky trace at a faster clip than either of the fat horses had traveled in years.

III

Goat Springs in the late forenoon was a lazy place. People kept out of the sun, loafing in the shade of the slat awnings or in the shadowed interiors of the stores. Hardly a soul moved on the main street as Faith, still standing, turned the flying carriage in from the Gulch road and spun

down the three dusty blocks to pull to a jerky halt before the newspaper office.

She jumped out, heedless of the fact that the hem of her ruffles caught on the high step and that for a full minute the embroidered edges of her muslin drawers were distinctly visible to the interested loafers under the awning of Gettler's store.

She didn't wait to tether the team, but they were so beat out by their unaccustomed run that they were content to stand, heads down, blowing softly. She started into the newspaper office, then paused, turned, and went back after the carriage whip.

The bright glare of the sunny street had dimmed her eyes so that the shadowed interior of the print shop seemed almost dark and for a moment she thought the place deserted. Then movement behind the homemade type cases proved her error as Mark Gorman straightened from the box on which he had been sitting to stare at his visitor in open-mouthed surprise.

"Why, Miss Thorndyke!"

"I'll Miss Thorndyke you!" she yelled. She'd forgotten that her grandmother said ladies never raised their voices. At the moment she was all Gus Thorndyke's daughter, and, whatever old Gus's faults, hesitation was not among them. She took a better grip on the carriage whip and swung it with both hands.

Marcus Gorman could move fast for a big man. He stepped backward quickly to escape the swirling lash, caught his heel on the box that had been his seat, and fell heavily. His head struck against the iron frame of the press as he went down, and blood spattered from a break in the top of his scalp. The fall did not put him out, but he was thoroughly stunned, as much from surprise as from the bump.

He stayed there, helpless, half sitting, half lying, one foot up on the overturned box, the other doubled under him. Faith came around the type case at a half gallop and stood over him, brandishing her whip, every inch of her four foot, eleven and three-quarters quivering with unsuppressed indignation.

"Hold a lady up to ridicule, will you! Call me names, you sniveling liar. I'll teach you to write about me in your newspaper, and, when you do, I'll teach you to spell the words right. I'll teach you to call me a dragon. I'll show you what a dragon really is."

Marcus Gorman moved one hand tentatively as the whip jerked its warning. He stayed where he was, his slightly addled senses slowly coming back to normal, but he couldn't repress a smile. The girl was so very small, and so very mad, and so very pretty. He watched her eyes that had turned almost black and gave her a couple of minutes to cool off.

Finally he raised a hand slowly and tested the bump on his head. "Can I get up now?"

Faith Thorndyke didn't know exactly what to do. She was a little surprised at herself as reaction set in, and considerably shaken. She had expected him to fight back, to curse her, at least. But you couldn't whip a man who merely lay quietly on his back, even if he was as big as all get out. She answered by retreating a couple of steps, and he untangled his legs carefully and rose, again gingerly exploring the knot on his skull.

"I guess I was right. You certainly act just like old Gus would."

Her eyes darkened again as anger surged up. "Apparently that isn't a compliment, coming from you."

"It's not," he told her honestly as he towered above her.

"You seem much better at calling names than paying compliments," she said bitterly. "I hope you're very proud of yourself for what you wrote about me, and on my wedding day, too!"

He shifted uncertainly from one foot to the other. This girl was the most disconcerting person he had ever met. There was a bucket of water in the corner. He found a rag and used it to swab the blood out of his hair.

She marched over to stand defiantly in front of him, kicking back the dragging ruffle of her skirt. "It's lucky for you Lazarus isn't in town. He wouldn't have come here with a whip . . . he'd have brought a gun."

He didn't seem properly impressed, so she went on heatedly. "Just because he's peace-loving and doesn't go in for street brawls and such doesn't mean that he's frightened by you. He might stand for a lot of things, but he certainly wouldn't let you get away with insulting me in print. When he reads that wedding story, he'll probably blow you right out of town."

Gorman's eyebrows went up in surprise. Then he walked over to the makeshift desk and picked half a dozen papers from the file he kept there. "I guess you haven't seen these, but I assure you that the rest of your crowd has, including Lazarus. I thought it had taken you a powerful long time to come and see me."

She stared at the smudgy sheets, realizing that these were the issues that had been printed since her arrival in camp. She read swiftly, her mouth tightening into a white line.

He'd begun by expressing the hope that the newly arrived Faith Thorndyke was a better sport than her father had been and that she would give the miners a better break and let a little of the mine's wealth trickle into their pockets. The second week he had told his readers that apparently the hope was unfounded, that the mining company was proceeding with its old hoggish, selfish policy. The third, he began to mention stock rigging and to hint that something was false in the rising value of Consolidated shares. In the fourth and fifth issues he called names:

> Lazarus Howe is up to his old tricks. The mine is about played out, and Lazarus is looking around for a sucker to unload it on.
>
> The trouble is that he can't find a sucker with sufficient funds. The only other way out is to sell the worthless stock to the miners. But since the miners all work underground, they know that the ore in the main vein is failing. Therefore friend Lazarus is trying a trick. He's started a new tunnel, a very secret tunnel that only a picked crew is allowed to enter. He's started rumors that the new tunnel is leading into a new bonanza, and, since miners aren't very smart, they're falling for the trick that Lazarus and his new female boss are pulling.

The girl looked up, her eyes snapping. "You must have hated my father very much to make such terrible statements about me."

Marcus Gorman shook his head. "I didn't hate old Gus. Tell you the truth, I kind of half admired the old reprobate. He was a thieving crook, but he never tried to euchre the men working for him on a stock-selling scheme."

"And you think I am?"

"Aren't you?" They stared at each other stiffly, and he added: "Maybe I've got it wrong. Maybe you're just under Lazarus's thumb and . . ."

"I'm under no man's thumb."

"Sure you are. Marrying Lazarus gives him a chance to cash in by selling your worthless stock. Don't you see it? Without you, Lazarus couldn't gain a thing by going through with this deal. But you're the perfect set-up for him, the fall guy. And he certainly ain't fit to be any woman's husband."

She was so angry that it was hard to speak. "And I suppose you think you are?"

He was genuinely distressed. "Who, me? Oh, that wasn't what I meant. I honestly never gave that a thought." He reddened. "I'm not what you might term a marrying man."

Realizing she'd gotten personal, Faith Thorndyke could have bitten out her tongue. "A newspaper editor is not God," she told him tartly. "You have apparently set yourself up as arbiter of everything that goes on in Goat Springs, telling me who I shouldn't marry and all. Have you always thought you were smarter than anyone else in the world?"

He stirred uncomfortably under her words. She could change the subject faster than a Philadelphia lawyer. "It's not me," he said, wondering why he felt that he had to explain. "It's that danged printing press. Ever since I met that tramp printer down at the Silver Dollar, I've been in trouble."

"You didn't have to play cards with him."

"Well"—he spoke slowly as if puzzled by the whole situation—"it wouldn't have been courteous not to. I was sure disappointed when I found I'd won nothing but an old press and some type."

"Which you probably stole."

"Lady," he said, "you never saw that printer play cards. I had to work real hard to beat him. It took almost all night, and I've wished, a hundred times since, I'd lost. That press drives me crazy. It's just like a conscience you don't want. I hadn't any more than started the paper when people came running to tell me things that weren't any of my business. Before I got it, I tended strictly to my own affairs. If I got sick of one camp, I just loaded the burros and we wandered to another. But now I'm hog-tied, minding chores for the whole town."

"And writing lies," she snapped, "like accusing me of swindling the miners into buying worthless stock. I haven't sold anybody anything, and besides Consolidated stock isn't worthless. The mine is very rich."

The printer rubbed his ear, looking at her doubtfully. "Somebody's been selling the stock . . . a lot of it . . . and, if you don't know about it, you'd better ask Mister Lazarus Howe some pointed questions."

"Are you implying that Lazarus is selling my stock without telling me about it? I don't believe you."

He sounded stubborn. "All I know is three things . . . the brokers, who handle Lazarus's business, are selling a wagonload of stock, the miners are telling me the main workings are about played out, but they're excited over this new tunnel. They're buying shares right and left. It smells to me like Lazarus is pulling a fast caper. Why should he be selling if they'd just found a new bonanza?"

She said: "But this is silly. Why don't you just go and look at the new tunnel? It seems to me that, if I were running a newspaper, I'd find out the facts before I wrote a story."

"There!" he said. "There!" He stooped and put his face down level with hers. "I've been trying for three solid weeks to get into that shaft without killing somebody."

Faith Thorndyke shook the whip in his face. "I'll get you into the shaft and without killing anyone, either. I've never heard anything so absurd in my life. And when you've seen how rich it is, are you a big enough man to apologize to Lazarus for what you said in your newspaper?"

"Ma'am," he said, "I'll give it the whole front page. I'll start it off . . . 'The Editor Is a Liar.' That satisfy you?"

She nodded, hitched up the ruffled skirt, and headed determinedly for the door. Mark Gorman loosened his heavy gun, spun the cylinder, and then followed her into the sunlight.

The loafers across the street grew wide-eyed as he helped her into the carriage. Mark Gorman knew that their tongues were already wagging. His printed feud with the owner of the Consolidated had been followed by Goat Springs with growing delight. And now he was riding away at her side, in her carriage, and she was wearing her wedding dress. It would be enough fuel to keep the gossips going for months.

The fat horses, refreshed by their rest, stepped out briskly, prancing through the dust of Main Street as it followed the contour of the hill and dropped down through the section known locally as Roaring Gulch. Here the character of the business changed, substantial stores giving place to rag-tail saloons, shooting galleries, and cheap dance halls that struggled with each other for space along the rocky hillsides.

Faith Thorndyke always shuddered as she traveled through this part of town. She sat, rigid and blushing, wishing desperately that she didn't have on a bridal dress. She had forgotten all about it in her rush, and now the whole population of Roaring Gulch streamed out. Gamblers appeared in saloon doorways to be joined by bartenders, still wearing their aprons, and a whole medley of greetings poured at Gorman as they passed. It was worse than a shivaree.

Even Gorman seemed a little embarrassed and quickened the horses' pace, but he couldn't escape his companion's waspish comment. "You seem to have a very wide acquaintance, Mister Editor."

He shifted uncomfortably under her scorn. "In my business you know people. News is not made solely by the upper classes. In fact, their doings are strangely uninteresting."

"But you printed enough about me." She had made her point and felt very pleased. "You didn't really know anything about me, and yet you printed in the paper that I was a thieving, grasping woman."

Marcus Gorman couldn't think of anything to say. The girl looked so small and helpless and young, but he had an uneasy suspicion that maybe she was smarter than he was.

IV

The road came out of the gulch onto the flat volcanic rock and he turned toward the mine head frame that reared up above the lower buildings.

From the offices on the right, the superintendent appeared as Gorman swung the carriage around and jumped down.

Titus Creig didn't see the girl. She was still in the seat and the curtained back obscured his view. He was short and square and weathered and his voice was rough with anger. "You've been warned to keep off this property, Mark. You know Mister Howe's orders as well as I do."

Gorman was a good head taller. He turned and smiled down at the short man. "Slow down a minute, Creig. I'm here to have a look below at the personal invitation of your boss."

Titus shook his head. "I know that Howe never told you to go underground and never will. What are you trying to do . . . pull a fast one while he's away?"

"I didn't say Howe told me." Gorman was unhurried but watchful. "I said your boss did." He swung around the carriage and offered the girl his hand.

Creig's eyes widened at the sight of Faith Thorndyke stepping to the ground. He started to speak, then stopped, his eyes narrowing, taking in the dress, recognizing it as his wife's. Something had happened that he did not understand, and caution kept him speechless.

Faith smiled, seeing his look. "I'm hardly dressed for it, Mister Creig, but this is important. We're going into the mine. I'm here to prove to Mister Gorman that he's been lying about us all."

Creig swallowed slowly, trying to think. Marcus Gorman had moved back, leaving them to face each other, smiling a little to himself as he found the situation highly entertaining.

Creig was in a spot. He was a fairly simple man, and average honest. He knew what Lazarus Howe had been doing and saw nothing very wrong. The creed of his existence was that you looked out for yourself. But he dared not let Gorman underground, for the editor knew ore and mining practice, and, if he once saw the face of the new tunnel, the fat was in the fire.

The girl seemed unaware of his hesitation. She said: "There seems to be some misunderstanding here. Mister Gorman says that you've prevented him from entering the mine."

"It isn't practice to let strangers into the workings," Creig tried to temporize, "especially when they happen to be newspapermen."

"That's exactly why I want him to see the workings for himself." Faith Thorndyke's voice had grown a little heated. "He's made some utterly ridiculous charges. I want them retracted. I want to prove to him that he's not only mistaken in what he's written, but that he's made a perfect fool of himself."

The men exchanged quick glances. Gorman's eyes were mocking, Creig's harried and uncertain.

He hedged. "Well, I don't think it's wise for you to accompany us." He had no clear picture of what he meant to do, but if he could get Gorman into the mine alone, he might find a solution. Maybe an accident . . .

But the girl forestalled this at once. "Are you trying to keep me from entering my own mine, Mister Creig?"

"Of course not," he said hastily. Her level eyes disconcerted him; they reminded him of old Gus. "It isn't that at all, but miners are a superstitious lot. They think it's bad luck for a woman to go underground. They don't like it. I've known them to quit for no better reason."

Her small chin set stubbornly. "They'll just have to get over it. I'm going down. I wouldn't miss seeing the sheepish look on Mister Gorman's face when he has his first look at the new vein."

Gorman chuckled softly. "I guess it's up to you, Creig. Fish or cut bait."

The superintendent looked at Gorman and knew that he had lost, but he made one last attempt. "At least wait until Lazarus gets back," he pleaded. "You don't want to make it harder for us to keep labor in the mine. You apparently don't believe me, but you'll believe Lazarus and . . ."

"We're going down now," the girl told him, without glancing at her companion. "I certainly don't want to give Mister Gorman the chance to say that I promised to show him the workings, and then changed my mind."

For an instant it seemed that Creig would bar her physically from the buildings, then he shrugged and ushered her into the office.

Equipped with a cap and a miner's lamp, but still wearing the wedding dress, Faith Thorndyke looked tinier than ever as they moved into the shaft house and stepped into the suspended cage.

Creig had tried to stop at the door, but Marcus Gorman laughed gently.

"Get in!" Gorman had a persuasive way of speaking although he did not raise his voice. The superintendent stepped in. Gorman followed. The gate clanged and the cage dropped with breath-robbing suddenness.

Faith Thorndyke felt her knees turn jelly-like. She thought the rest of her body would never catch up. It was like riding a matchbox suspended in nothingness on an elastic string. Then they stopped as suddenly as the drop had begun, seeming to bounce for a full minute before the cage came to rest. Gorman released the gate, and they stepped out into the workings.

The station at the 300-foot level had been carved from the living rock. The main haulage tunnel led away upward on a one percent grade for drainage purposes, disappearing like the entrance to a dark cave beyond the circle of their flickering lights.

Faith crowded down her rising panic and turned to the left where a wooden bulkhead had been built to block a second tunnel. The bulkhead stood open now for ventilation, but was guarded by a man who sat on a small wooden platform with a check sheet before him and a gun strapped to his hip. He rose as they moved toward him.

Creig said: "This is Miss Thorndyke, Baxter. She wants to inspect the new workings."

The guard was a tall man with a skinny neck and

a prominent Adam's apple that moved up and down when he spoke. His bold eyes showed pale, even whitish in the uncertain light. "Sorry." He didn't sound sorry. "You know the orders."

Gorman could not tell whether some hidden signal had passed between the men, but Creig was obviously relieved. "You see how it is," he told the girl. "Even I can't enter that tunnel without a direct order from Lazarus Howe."

"I can," she said. "I own this mine and I intend to inspect it." She walked slowly toward the guard, expecting him to give passage.

Baxter's narrow, fish-like mouth tightened, and he said distinctly: "Don't try it, lady. You'll get hurt."

Faith Thorndyke had never seen a professional gunman before, but suddenly she knew that this thin man with the low husky voice would not hesitate to use any method to stop her. The knowledge only made her more determined to enter that tunnel. She tossed her head, switching back the light veil that floated in the draft. The guard put out his left hand and grasped her shoulder, and what happened next was too rapid for her to understand clearly.

Marcus Gorman brushed her roughly out of the way and seized the guard's right wrist, jerking the man forward, twisting him until the guard was faced half away, then dropping him to his knees as Baxter struggled to reach his holstered gun.

Gorman was bigger and heavier, yet for an instant their strengths seemed so evenly matched that there was not movement of any kind.

Then slowly the imprisoned wrist was pushed up between Baxter's shoulder blades, and he bent forward, still struggling, cursing in a monotonous undertone until there was a sharp snap and he cried out shrilly in sudden pain.

Gorman released his grip, lifted the gun from its holster, and stepped back, slipping the captured weapon into his own waistband.

Baxter groveled on the floor, moaning with a little slobbering sound, his arm hanging, disjointed and limp, at his side. Faith Thorndyke watched him in utter disbelief, then turned shocked eyes toward the big editor. Both Gorman and the mine superintendent were motionless, watching each other. As she looked, Creig raised his hands a little away from his body, palms out, in a gesture that was entirely plain. This fight was none of his.

But the girl was not appeased. "You broke his arm. You purposely broke his arm."

Gorman's attention turned to the writhing guard. "You wanted in that tunnel, didn't you?"

"But it wasn't necessary to break his arm. You had him powerless. You just had a sadistic desire to prove how strong you are. A little boy, showing off again."

He shook his head sharply. "No, I know how strong I am. There's something you've got to learn, ma'am. In this country you don't change your mind once you're started. It wouldn't have helped to take Baxter's gun. He'd have found another one, then I'd have to kill him. He may cool off a little before it heals."

Without a further word she brushed ahead into the new tunnel and the two men followed her. The tunnel was only 200 yards long, and they came up against the face to find four miners mucking broken rock into a handcar.

The apparition of the girl in the white dress froze their sweaty, dirt-streaked faces in sudden fear until Titus Creig came up behind her. Then they relaxed, giving back, sullen and resentful, leaning on their shovels as Gorman climbed upon the broken rock to have a better look at the face.

He looked mockingly at Creig. "So, this is the mysterious vein we've been hearing so much about."

The superintendent said morosely: "No one connected with the mine claimed there was a new vein. As far as I know, this tunnel is just for development work."

"There have been plenty of rumors." Gorman glanced at the silent girl. "The Consolidated stock has been selling around twenty cents because of them."

One of the watching miners snickered, and Creig said angrily: "I'm not responsible for rumors,

Mark Gorman. You know that you can hear any-thing where mining is concerned."

"I can recognize a rigged market when I see one." Gorman turned fully to the girl, his courtesy a little exaggerated. "Thank you for allowing me underground."

Faith Thorndyke knew nothing about mining, but she knew from the way Creig spoke, the attitude of the miners, and Gorman's manner that something was very wrong. But the stubbornness which was the direct inheritance from her father made her refuse to give up, even yet.

When they reached the surface, Gorman asked the privilege of examining their mill reports.

"Show him anything he wants to see," she said. "We can't allow him to think that we've refused to co-operate."

Creig had given up what he knew to be a hopeless fight. He shrugged wearily and led them into the mine office, and produced the books. Even to an amateur it was obvious that the mill returns had been decreasing steadily and for the last two months they had barely covered the freight and penalties. The mine was operating at a huge loss, a loss that could not continue long, since the cash reserves were practically exhausted.

Titus Creig said in a strained voice: "You aren't going to publish this are you, Mark? You'll kill the camp overnight."

"It seems to me," said Gorman, his face

expressionless, "that Goat Springs is already dead and just doesn't know it. You haven't enough money in the bank to more than meet this week's payroll. What were you planning to do then, shut down?"

Creig spread his hands wordlessly, and Gorman motioned to the girl. "Look at the books, Miss Thorndyke, and see whether I've been telling the truth. I'd guess that your friend, Lazarus, hoped to get out of here as soon as the wedding was over. The mine is through. It will have to close, unless you get outside help, and no one will advance money on the strength of the present showing."

She was examining the books, and spoke without looking up. "And the town?"

"Will die," he said. "They get their water from the mine. In a few days, there won't be a town here."

She thought: *I should have known this all the time. I should have asked questions and found out.* The knowledge made her angry with herself, but she was even angrier at Gorman. The big ox was always right.

She fought back a sudden rush of tears, and took charge. "You'll close the mine tonight," she told Creig. "You'll see that the men are paid." Then she turned and fled out of the office.

She had turned the horses and was heading for the road before Gorman caught her, vaulting over the moving wheel to the seat at her side.

"What are you going to do?" Mark asked her.

43

She refused to let him take the reins. She kept her eyes steadily on the backs of the moving horses. "I'm going to buy back every share of stock that Lazarus has sold the miners by trickery."

Shocked surprise stiffened Gorman's big frame. "Wait a minute. Let's not get excited. I know that this has all come suddenly to you, but you've got to consider. The mine is closed. You're buying a dead horse and . . ."

"I know what I'm doing." The words were grim. "I know I can't buy up every share of stock in the mine, but I can buy those that Lazarus peddled dishonestly. I certainly don't want the miners' money. What else could I do, Mister Editor? You always seem to have an answer for everything."

"It will probably take every cent you have."

She sat ramrod straight on the lurching seat. "Then I'll go back to my grandfather's where I came from."

"Do you want to go back?"

She knew that she didn't. This country had put its mark upon her. "What's that got to do with it?" she demanded. "Certainly you of all people don't expect me to keep the money that was robbed from the miners?"

He squirmed under the bite of her words. "Look, you've got it wrong. I'm not telling you what you should do, I just thought . . ."

"Didn't you put what you thought in that newspaper . . . or were you just wasting ink?"

"Well, that was before I knew you and . . ."

"I let Lazarus sell that stock because I was too careless to find out what was going on. I'm not blaming him. I don't know why he did it."

"I can tell you," Gorman said. "He meant to marry you and . . ."

"I'm not interested. If I'd paid attention, it couldn't have happened, so I'm going to buy those shares back. I'll probably need your help, and, since you chose to butt in, I guess you owe me that much. Once I'm finished buying the stock, I'll be very glad to say good bye, both to you and to Goat Springs."

The horses had plodded their way through Roaring Gulch and reached the main section of town before he said: "Won't you wait until Lazarus gets back? Let him handle things and . . ."

"It's too late," she said, turning to look at him. "If you're going to hold the public conscience, Mister Editor, you have to be tough enough to go through with your program even when the going gets rough."

His tone was as bitter as hers had been. "I've held my last public conscience. I'm going to leave the press in Goat Springs. I'm tired of living with other people's worries. I'm tired of feeling guilty because I butted into their affairs. I'll never do it again."

"Running away!" She couldn't resist the gibe.

"Just taking back my freedom," he said, hoping

it was true and knowing it wasn't. No matter where he went he was never going to get this girl out of his mind. He tried to think of a way to tell her, but there was no time for they had already reached the bank.

V

Martin Eaton had been a cowboy before he wandered into Tonopah with the first rush and shared a bed with Gus Thorndyke on a rocky hillside. That accident of sleeping accommodations developed his friendship with the old boss and turned him into a banker when Goat Springs started. Everything he had he owed to Thorndyke, and he was genuinely distressed by what the girl told him.

He said finally: "I don't know whether you realize that, before Lazarus began selling your stock, your bank balance was down to practically nothing. Your dad loved to spend money. The house cost a fortune, so did the hotel and this bank building."

"That's all beside the point." Faith Thorndyke shrugged.

"And what makes you think the miners will sell the stock back to you? They're a suspicious lot. They may think this some kind of a trick."

"Mister Gorman will tell them."

The banker glanced at the big editor without liking. "He's been telling them in his newspaper and yet they keep buying."

"Then they can go to the mine and look for themselves."

He tried another track. "I don't know how much you know about the town affairs. Outside of your account and the mill account, there's little in this bank. If you close your account, we close our doors."

"The mine is shutting down at sunset," she said. "I understand that without the mine the town is finished, so what difference does it make?"

The banker gave up sadly. "What is it that you want me to do?"

"How many shares have been sold since the new tunnel started?"

"About half a million."

She was staggered by the number. "How much are they worth?" Her voice sounded weak.

He looked at a note on his desk. "They closed this noon at twenty-one cents."

She steadied herself, one hand on the corner of his desk. "What is the balance of my account?"

He called across the big room to the cashier, and the man brought over a slip of paper on which he had written some figures. The banker's tone was dry as sand. "You have exactly one hundred and two thousand, three hundred and sixty-two dollars, and thirteen cents."

Faith Thorndyke wet her lips and repeated the figure aloud. She had no real conception of money in large sums and this figure sounded very large. "Could I have it in cash, please?"

The banker hesitated. "You'd better give them checks. We'll stay open until the last one is cashed." He sighed a little, then reached out for her small hand. He held it up, chuckling at the incongruity of its size against the power it was about to wield, and his face cleared.

"Funny thing, I guess I never really liked being tied to a bank chair, but I wish Gus could have lived to see this. Gus was a man that could laugh at a joke, even if it was on him."

The front door burst open, and Lazarus hurried in, calling the banker's name. He was dust-stained and so excited that he did not see Gorman or the girl, standing in the shadowed corner of the room.

"Martin! Hey, Martin! There's a new strike at Golden, fifty miles from here. I almost killed the horses getting back. I saw some of the ore at Rhyolite. It's picture rock and free milling. We'll take every dollar over there, get in on the ground floor, and . . ." He stopped, suddenly realizing the banker was not alone, and came forward, staring from the girl to Gorman.

"Faith, what are you doing here?"

She told him in a weary voice. She told him the whole story, without recriminations or anger. She told him how they had examined the tunnel and the books. She told him of her decision to repurchase the stock.

He stood, staring at her, his whole world falling apart at his feet, and his face turned stubborn and nasty. "I won't let you. I won't let you make a fool of all of us."

Gorman said quietly: "Don't interfere."

Lazarus turned to look at him, and there was hate in the smaller man's eyes, and also fear. "Keep out of this, you fool!"

The banker caught his breath. He expected Gorman to strike. Gorman was a little surprised that he didn't. Perhaps it was the girl.

He said, still speaking quietly: "And you're not going to Golden. If I find you there, or at any other of the southern camps, I'll run you out. It's your kind that's given the country a bad name. I mean it! Show up in Golden and I'll kill you."

The girl remembered the gun guard in the mine tunnel, the way Gorman had broken his arm, and she shuddered. Apparently Lazarus Howe saw the look on her face. He had opened his mouth to answer Gorman. He closed it slowly.

"Get going," said Gorman. "When the miners find out that the mine is about to close, they might come looking for you."

Howe went. Where he went, none in Goat Springs ever knew. All that they did know was that he failed to show up in Golden or in any other of the camps.

VI

Most mining towns die lingering deaths, but Goat Springs died with a flourish. When the mine shut down, it was the end of the water company, and without water none could live on the rocky hillsides.

With this in mind, the camp's last night was one prolonged howl. The gin mills and dance halls ran until dawn, selling their whiskey at cut rates since it would not pay to haul them across the desert, and Roaring Gulch rang with shouts until daylight. Then its bedraggled citizens headed out in any conveyance they could find, trailing off to new strikes, leaving the dying town behind them.

In the main section of Goat Springs the lights burned as brightly as they did in Roaring Gulch, and in the stock exchange, off the hotel lobby, Faith Thorndyke stood upon a chair, still wearing her bridal costume, and bought and bought and bought.

At first the brokers had kept aside, shocked by the news that the mine was closed, then, as they began to catch the spirit of festivity that ran through the town, they joined the strange revelry and, producing their office records, came forward to help.

Someone found a red tin trunk, placing it behind

the girl's chair, its bell lid thrown back. Into this they tossed the purchased shares carelessly. At first business was slow, but, as news of the doings spread, the street before the hotel was filled with pushing, shouting miners, angry and fearful of being shut out from the unexpected windfall.

As the early sellers began to filter through the crowd, waving their checks, the curses were replaced by laughter and the street gained a carnival air, while inside the long narrow room grew hot and close and smoke-filled as the seemingly never-ending line snaked its way forward slowly.

Gorman stood at the door, his big body a screen, his gun hanging ready as he weeded out the phonies, the men who tried to lie about the price they'd paid for their stock. He called each applicant by name, asked who the man's broker was, and the date of the stock purchase, then called the broker and searched the records. Not until he was satisfied did her permit the miner to enter.

But it was the girl, seeming to float like a white robed angel in the smoke haze, who was the center of the show. Personally she received each bunch of shares and personally she wrote each check, balancing it against the dwindling account.

As the night progressed, her face grew paler and paler with fatigue until it was as white as the wedding dress, but she never faltered although both the brokers and Gorman begged her to step down so they could take her place.

"This is the one thing that will be done right," she said grimly. "I'll know it was done properly because I'm going to stay and do it myself." And stay she did until the last share had been bought, the last check written, and only a few dollars remained in her account.

When darkness faded into morning light, the town was already half deserted. Some of the women cried as they rode down the rocky gulch. The mayor and his wife were gone, accompanied by the superintendent of the mine, but the banker, true to his word, lingered, seated alone in the vaulted room of the old building that Gus had built to last 100 years.

The floor was littered with the records of the camp's twenty-four rowdy months of life, records that would yellow and curl where they lay, gradually to be buried by the creeping dust.

Martin Eaton did not rise until he saw Faith Thorndyke emerge from the hotel, then, knowing that the sale was done, that the last check was cashed, he came to his feet, gathered up the small amount of cash from his desk, set his hat firmly on his head, and stepped out into the dawn.

He thrust the small wad of money into the girl's hand and, after a moment's hesitation, turned the other way and walked slowly toward his house where his wife was already packing.

The street was filled with moving wagons. A horse was worth $1,000 gold that morning, and none for sale. Those who lacked other transportation used wheelbarrows, baby carriages, or carried what they could on their backs.

Two brokers followed Faith Thorndyke from the hotel, carrying between them the red tin trunk. They loaded it into the carriage boot, stepped back, tipped their hats, and moved away to arrange their own departure.

Gorman had the girl's arm, steadying her. He looked up and down the busy street, seeing family after family pass. But he did not wave, and they offered no good byes. The celebration of the night was buried in the cold ashes of departure, and the moving picture filled him with a deep sadness.

"I'm sorry it had to end this way," he said, perplexed. "I'm sorry I ever wrote about you in the paper. By noon this crowd will be halfway to Golden, ready to fight each other for a new stake. Maybe you spent your money for nothing."

"No." Faith sounded very tired. "I learned something last night. I learned that owning things leads to responsibility, and I'm not certain I like responsibility. I'm almost glad the mine is closed."

He nodded, frowning. "I know what you mean. That printing press has owned me ever since I won it."

"But now you're free, too," she said. "All you

have to do is to load your burros and pull out. Leave the press in Goat Springs, let it rust and fall apart with the rest of the camp. That's what you're going to do, isn't it?"

"Of course," he said. "Of course, that's what I'm going to do."

"Then help me into the carriage, please."

He took her small hand and helped her up into the high seat. As she stepped in, the ruffles of the long dress caught under the step and tore with a sharp, ripping sound. She sat, looking down at the tear that extended half across the front of the dress, and two tears forced their way from under her lids and ran slowly down her cheeks.

Gorman saw the tears and tried to say something but a lump caught in his throat. The girl did not wait. She seized the reins, backed the horses around sharply, and wheeled them up the street, cutting through the steady stream of wagons coming down the hill.

Gorman stood still until the carriage reached the track and turned up the rougher trail toward the house at the head of the gulch. When it was lost to sight, he about-faced and slowly marched into the hotel.

VII

In the big house on the hill, Myra Perkins let the exhausted girl sleep until ten o'clock. The housekeeper was not emotional and this was not the first mining camp she had seen die. She packed systematically, with an eye to the load that the carriage could haul.

She considered the silver doorknobs and decided that they weren't worth their weight. She hesitated over the crayon portrait of old Gus, and finally left it hanging in the place of honor above the mantel.

But she did choose many things—the crystal candelabra, the silver chest—loading them until the carriage springs flattened and the bed rested firmly on the axle beneath.

Then she waked the girl, standing for a moment looking down at her, curled in the big, four-poster bed.

Faith Thorndyke still wore the torn wedding dress. She had been so tired that she had made no effort to remove it. She opened her eyes at Myra's touch and stared for an instant, uncomprehending, not knowing where she was. Then she saw the housekeeper and her face cleared. She reached out, grasping the older woman's hand, thanking her silently.

Myra said gruffly: "It's time to be moving, miss. We should have started hours ago, but I couldn't bear to wake you. It will be hot across the desert, and it's a long way to Rhyolite."

Faith nodded as she rose. She changed into a more suitable costume, looking sadly at the torn white dress. Only yesterday it had been so beautiful. She made no protest as Myra pointed out the things that must be left.

"We could hire a couple of wagons," the housekeeper said, "only there ain't a wagon for hire in the whole camp. You might send back for the stuff, but I doubt you ever will. People seldom do. They mean to, but somehow they never get around to it."

Faith did not answer. She walked slowly through the big rooms having her last look. She had her last drink from the faucet in the kitchen sink since there was still water in the tin tank, and then she followed Myra outside, closing the door.

The red tin trunk lay on the ground where Myra had hauled it from the boot, and Faith stopped. "That goes," she said.

The older woman tried to argue, pointing to the load, but Faith was firm. "I don't care if the carriage is full. Throw something out. I know it's nothing but worthless paper, but I want to keep those shares. I want something to remind myself that I once owned a mine."

Myra Perkins knew when to argue and when to

56

hold her peace. She rearranged the load and between them they lifted the trunk to the rear carriage seat. Then they harnessed the horses, since the Indian boy had gone.

With Myra driving, they started down the rocky trail. The housekeeper did not urge the horses. She was wise to the ways of the country and she knew they had a long way to go.

The road they traveled was empty, the houses on each side already deserted. Lace curtains still blew from open windows, and, where doors stood gaping, the rooms within showed furnished and livable as if their owners had stepped out but for a minute.

A ghostly unreal quiet lay across the camp. They passed the mayor's house and Creig's and the banker's establishment, and so turned into the main street.

Some of the store buildings were shuttered and closed; other owners had taken what goods could be transported, leaving the litter of their departure in a jumbled mass upon the sidewalks.

For a moment Faith thought that they were alone in the empty town, and then she saw the curious rig pulled up before the newspaper office, and, as she watched, Marcus Gorman appeared struggling under the weight of the hand press.

Unconscious that he had an audience, he set it on the ground, got a better grip, and managed somehow to raise it to the wagon bed. The wagon was a sorry affair, a discard obviously, its rusty tires wired to the sunken wheels, its bed swayback and so weak that the press made it sag in the middle until the rough boards touched the reach, bending it toward the ground.

Gorman surveyed it calculatingly, so engrossed in his task that he did not notice the approach of the carriage. He turned then and went back after the type cases, hefting them, drawers and all, despite the weight. He was just loading the last when Faith Thorndyke pulled the carriage alongside and made the horses pause.

Looking around quickly, Gorman removed his hat, wiping the sweat from his forehead. "Hello. I thought everyone had gone."

"We're just leaving." The girl held her place, staring beyond him at the four disconsolate burros standing in their makeshift harness before the canted wagon. "Do you think they can pull it?"

He shrugged, none too hopefully. "We'll see."

"I thought you were going to leave the press here?"

His grin was a little sheepish. "I meant to. I started out with the burros two hours ago and every step I took I knew I was running away. I decided that I wasn't going to be a fugitive from a printing press for the rest of my life, so I came back. Besides, they'll probably need a paper at Golden and . . ."

At first he thought she was crying, and in

sudden consternation ran to the carriage. But Faith Thorndyke was laughing. She laughed, long and hard, and when at last she could, she said: "All right, let's see what those burros can do."

He hesitated, looking back at the newspaper office for a moment, then he picked up the lines and chirped to the burros. Nothing happened. He went around in front and tried to lead them, but they tightened the traces and then refused to budge.

He gave up finally and shrugged. "I guess the little beasts have better sense than I have. I guess I shouldn't have come back. I guess the press stays here, after all."

Faith Thorndyke didn't answer. She jumped down from the carriage and began to unhitch her team.

Gorman stared at her in disbelief. "Wait, you can't do that."

"Shut up and help me," she told him.

"But everything you own is in that carriage."

"Those things aren't important." She had the traces free. "Get those silly burros out of the way. Why is it a man can never do anything right by himself?"

"But I can't let you leave your stuff, just for my press. . . ."

"It isn't your press," she spoke without looking at him. "We both should stop kidding ourselves. The press is the voice of the miners, of the people, here and in Golden, everywhere. It's a voice that has to be heard, that must keep on being heard. Don't you understand that, even yet?"

He looked at her, then meekly he loosened the burros and started to lead them around to hitch them at the rear of the wagon.

Myra Perkins stopped him. "Wait a minute," the housekeeper said. "I'm older than both of you put together, and the press is a good thing, but I've had to start life a lot of times in a lot of different towns, and it's nice to have a few things to help you along." She led the burros to the carriage and hitched them. "It isn't as heavy as the wagon," she said. "They can haul it. I'll drive them. You kids drive the wagon."

Faith was about to protest.

"And you'd better take that tent." Myra was pointing at the print shop. "Land sakes, if it wasn't for me, we wouldn't even have a roof over our heads."

Meekly Gorman went back and unfastened the canvas roof from its wooden frame. He rolled it, stowed the roll in the wagon behind the press. Then he mounted the seat and chirped to the horses and they rolled down the rocky grade, the last people to leave Goat Springs.

VIII

Golden sat in a bare, rocky cañon. Faith Thorndyke thought that, if she could only forget the long, dusty, burning, desert miles, she might easily imagine that they were actually in Goat Springs.

They pulled up the grade to find tent houses already spreading up along the main street. Gorman braked the wagon to a stop before a rocky piece of ground that no one had yet preëmpted. He unhitched the team and, going back, helped Myra Perkins unharness the burros. Then he lifted out the press and type cases, and broke up the wagon, using the resulting wood to build a rough frame over which he stretched the canvas roof. That done, he carried the press inside, and then unloaded the carriage.

He turned then to the girl, and his face was redder than she had ever seen it. "Look," he said, fumbling with his hat. "As we drove in, I saw the *padre* down the street. I . . . well . . . ."

"Sure, she will," said Myra Perkins. "Kiss her, you fool, and then go get that sky pilot."

Gorman kissed the girl. He was a little awkward. Then he hurried down the street. Faith looked after him, and there were tears in her eyes, but Myra was practical. "We should fix this place up a little. Wish I had something to cover the walls with."

Her eyes fell on the tin trunk and she opened it, bringing out the gaily colored certificates. They were pretty, all green and red and gold ink.

"At least," the woman muttered as she pinned them up, "old Gus did things right. When he bought anything, it was the best."

Faith had found the sign that Gorman had brought. She took a heavy crayon and marked out Goat Springs and put in Golden, then she hung the sign before the tent and stood back to read.

GOLDEN NEWS—JOB PRINTING
MARCUS GORMAN, EDITOR AND OWNER

Then she went in and put on her torn wedding dress and sat down to wait. Gorman and the *padre* didn't keep her waiting more than a few minutes.

Lost Gold

I

Bill Drake's crew rode into camp just before dark on that windy May day, fourteen trail-hardened men, not counting the bald-headed cook. They camped at the edge of the wash a full three miles north of Tucson, picketed their horses, put a guard out to watch them, and built a good fire against the coming night's chill.

While the cook threw the chuck together, they spread their blankets with the practiced ease of men who had lived most of their lives in the open, and then squatted around the fire, bearded and dust-caked from their long, weary days in the saddle.

Their eyes turned with unspoken longing toward the tiny cluster of lights that marked the town, for they had been on the trail three weeks, guarding a shipment of machinery that some fool was hauling southward into the Sierra Madre for a copper property he was trying to open. The crew was burned out and thirsting.

Bill Drake knew how they felt, but he had given the order as they rode up, and he meant it: "No one rides into town before I say so. I'll shoot the first brush-jumper I find in a saloon."

They had not liked the order, but Bill Drake had ears as sharp as a coyote's and there was no grumbling. They waited in gloomy silence until the chuck was ready, shivering in the blast of the chill wind coming down the draw from the distant peaks. Then they ate, turned morose and sullen by their thoughts of the town's pleasures that they were missing.

Only Andy Drake was foolhardy enough to question his brother's orders. Andy was a good inch shorter than his brother and twenty pounds lighter for all that he stood six-two and weighed 190.

"You're being a little rough," Andy said as he finished eating. He was conscious that the crew heard and watched him with concentrated attention. "The boys are weary and saddle galled. A night in town would do them no harm."

Bill Drake looked at him. Bill was not used to having his orders questioned by anyone. His squarish face set in hard lines and his blue eyes looked smoky.

"You run your business," he said, "and let me run mine. The town is full of yellowlegs, and, if I let the boys ride in, there will be half a dozen dead soldiers by morning. I've got no time to be arguing with the cavalry. Get your rifle, since you're so full of beans, and go out to relieve the horse guard. There are bronco Indians around and we don't want to lose our mounts."

He turned without further words and moved to the fire, leaving his younger brother to stare after

66

him in wordless anger, conscious of the veiled looks of amusement from the crew.

To them, Andy was an outsider even if he was Bill's brother, a kid who had ridden with them for less than three months. He picked up his rifle slowly and moved out, thinking bitterly: *I'm not Bill's slave. I've been in the saddle for days. I could use some liquor and maybe a woman. It would be fun to see a town again, something besides this cindery waste we've been riding through. I'd like to hear a piano, listen to laughter, see some lights and gaiety.*

He was tempted, after he relieved the horse guard, to cut out his own bay, saddle up, and ride in, but, instead, he moved along the rutted, sandy trail and sat on a rock a good 200 yards below the camp.

The broken ground behind him rose sharply toward the wash's rim, shadowed and eerie in the thin light from the distant moon. He stayed there, motionless, lost in the shadow, watching. He did not believe that an Indian would come this close to town. But with Apaches you never could tell. They might be anywhere.

The picketed horses stirred restlessly. Then above their shifting noise his quick ear caught the sound of someone riding toward him along the trail, the *clink* of metal ringing on a rock, someone riding a shod horse. No Indian, and probably not a Mexican. He rose and moved silently forward, shifting his rifle from the crook of his arm, keeping low so that he would not be outlined against the lighter sky. When the rider was directly opposite him, he stepped forward. "Pull up!" he said.

There was a low exclamation. Andy Drake almost dropped his gun. The rider was a woman. She checked her horse and sat motionlessly, watching him.

"Who . . . who are you?" she asked.

Andy recovered. "More to the point, who are you and what are you doing, riding this country alone at night? Only a fool would do that."

The girl did not relish being called a fool, but she was still nervous, still uncertain. "I'm . . . looking for Bill Drake."

Andy's surprise came back. As far as he knew, no one had any idea that Drake's crew was in this part of the country. Still, Bill never took anyone into his confidence, and he might well have arranged this meeting.

"And what would you be wanting with a mossback like Bill?"

She was not tall. Even on the back of her big roan she did not tower far above him. In the shadowed light he could see indistinctly that she wore a man's hat, low-crowned with a wide brim, men's trousers, and a brush jacket. Behind her saddle was a roll that he judged to be blankets, done up in a slicker. Certainly she looked as if she were set for travel, not just out for a pleasure ride. His curiosity grew, but her answer gave him no satisfaction.

"I'll discuss that with Bill Drake," she said steadily. "That fire marks his camp, doesn't it?"

"Could be," Andy said, still puzzled. "But I'm not certain Bill wants visitors."

"You might try asking." The girl's tone was short. "Tell him that Mister Wakeman sent me, and that it will be to his advantage if he talks to me."

Andy considered her in the half darkness. He had met the lawyer, Wakeman, and didn't like him. The man was too smooth, too certain of himself. He looked and acted more like a tinhorn gambler than a gentleman. But he was an associate of Bill's, at times arranging business for the outlaw.

"All right," Andy decided. "I guess one female isn't going to stampede the crew. Step off that horse and I'll take you in."

The girl dismounted, took the reins, and followed Andy toward the campfire. As she stepped out of the saddle, her brush jacket fell open and Andy caught a glint of a gun holstered at her waist. He had heard stories of women who wore men's clothes and rode with some of the outlaw bands, but he had never met one. He kept glancing across his shoulder at the girl, trying to size her up as they moved into the circle of light cast by the flickering fire. But it was hard to see her face, shadowed as it was by the low-drawn brim of her flat hat. He motioned for her to halt, and then moved around to where Bill Drake was talking to the bald-headed cook.

"What's this?" Bill was seldom surprised, but he was surprised now, and Andy drew a small feeling of comfort from the knowledge that his older brother could at times be caught off balance. There was, within Andy, a lurking sense of humor that he managed to keep hidden from the world, but a glint of it showed in his dark eyes as he faced Bill.

"A little lady," he said, "come out from town to hunt you with a message from Wakeman." He turned and motioned the girl forward, then added: "I didn't get her name."

"It's Mary," said the girl. "Mary Thorne." She still held the horse's reins as she faced the older brother. Her eyes studied his bearded face. "So you're Bill Drake?"

The outlaw's lips split in a half smile at her tone. "That's what they call me when they run out of worse names. What did Wakeman want, and how did he know we were here?"

"He saw you ride in at sunset."

Bill Drake's mouth twisted again. "That's Wakeman. Always watching, always sticking his nose into other people's business. Someday he'll get it chopped off short. What do you want to talk to me about?"

Mary Thorne's eyes strayed to the men circled around the fire, studying each for an instant in turn. They were bearded faces, dust-caked. None except the cook was old, yet their eyes had an aged wariness, a huntedness, as if none of them would ever be at ease.

They stared back at her, unmoving, unblinking, and in spite of herself she shivered a little. "I'd rather talk with you alone," she told Drake.

There was a snicker from the circle of watching men, and Bill Drake turned deliberately on his high heel. "Did anyone hear something funny?" His eyes raked their faces. The circle transferred its full attention from the girl to Drake, and Bill met their collective stare.

"Only a jackass laughs at nothing." His eyes dared them to pick up the fight, but none of them moved. He looked again at the girl, then at his brother. "Get back to the horses," he told Andy. "And you, ma'am, come around the cook wagon." He fastened the girl's horse to one of the wagon's high wheels.

As he did so, Mary Thorne glanced again at the circle of men, noting the hunger in their eyes, and the weight of their attention disturbed her. She glanced toward Andy in silent appeal as if asking him not to leave her alone in this camp.

Bill Drake saw the look, understood, and smiled. Bill Drake was quick at understanding people, at weighing them, and at guessing their hidden

71

thoughts and motives. It was this ability that had kept him alive during seven troubled years on the frontier. It was this that had made him the leader of the most dangerous crew that had ever ridden the badlands of the territory. He could meet force with force, craft with craft. He was ruthless when occasion indicated, but he could laugh. He chose to laugh now as he took the girl's arm.

His mocking eyes surveyed his brother across her shoulder. "Never mind. Andy won't be far away. Get moving, kid."

Andy gave him a long, studying look before he turned and vanished into the night, quiet as a shadow. Bill watched him with approval, and then led the girl around the wagon. Not until they reached its far side, screened from the fire by the high canvas cover, did he pause to speak.

"So you want something from me. Do you know what I am?"

She said: "I've heard them call you an outlaw."

Bill shrugged. He was not offended. "Most people who come into this hell-hole have broken the law . . . sometimes a lot of laws. It doesn't matter what I'm called so long as they leave me alone."

"I don't care what you are." Her voice was low, but steady and assured. "Mister Wakeman says you're the only white man who knows and will venture into the Superstition country."

Bill Drake's attention sharpened. He studied the

girl more carefully. She was small and the hair tucked up under the edge of her flat-crowned hat was a warm coppery brown. Her eyes were blue-green and, when she was intense, they darkened.

Drake took his time. "And what does anyone want to go into the Superstitions for? The cavalry gives it a wide berth, and even the Tonto and White Mountain Indians wouldn't be caught dead in that country. The only Indians who ever go into it are broncos, the outcasts, the wild ones, and whites. The whole place is supposed to be filled with evil spirits. Strange things happen in that country . . . things that no man can explain."

She was a little mocking. "Are you afraid of evil spirits?"

His grin was a little slow in coming. "The only evil spirits I'm afraid of is the liquor my crew loads up on in a saloon. It makes them harder to handle. But I wouldn't go into any bad country without good reason, and, as far as I know, there is no good reason to go anywhere near Superstition range."

"What about gold?"

He watched her. Then he started to chuckle. "Don't tell me you have an old Spanish map? Every saloon swamper north of Tombstone has one he'll sell you for three drinks."

"I have a map, all right. But it isn't Spanish and it's less than twenty years old. I know when it was drawn and who drew it. It shows the location of a wagon train that was burned in one of the draws leading down from Mount Superstition. That train was carrying over two hundred pounds of gold."

She sounded very positive, but Bill Drake shrugged. "I've heard every lost treasure story that's been told in the territory and I believe none of them. Certainly I'm not going to ride my crew through a hundred miles of the roughest country this side of hell merely on the strength of an old map. You can forget it, sister. Go tell your story to someone else."

Mary Thorne was startled. She was not used to men refusing her anything. It hadn't occurred to her that this outlaw would not jump at the chance of going after a trainload of gold. "You don't mean that?" Shock made her voice a little desperate. "You're a fool. The gold is there. My uncle drew this map, and he told me all about it. He was the only man who escaped from this train and lived . . . and . . ."

"Look." Bill Drake sounded as if he were trying to be patient. "You had a good look at the men around the fire. They're thieves, murderers, and cut-throats. The only reason they ride with me is because they know I'll lead them on no wild-goose chases. In this territory people call them Drake's private army. They're afraid of us, and the Indians leave us alone. We're more effective than the yellowlegs from Verde and Wingate and Apache. The stage company knows it, and the traders know it, and the mine owners know it. They pay us to guard their shipments, they pay us to bring stolen stock back from Mexico, and they pay us well. But no one will pay us for riding after your lost treasure."

"I'll pay you," said Mary Thorne. "You'll get a full share of the gold. You've just got to go. Mister Wakeman says the Indians have broken out of San Carlos, that no one is safe to cross the country unless they have a company of cavalry as a guard."

"That's right." Drake's lips quirked. "Why not try one of the forts? With that hair and those eyes any yellowleg officer would be a patsy for you. They'd probably order out the whole garrison."

"You!" She stamped her small foot in the dust. "It would serve you right if I did get someone else. But I'm not going to. I'm going to have you go with me, Mister Bill Drake. Do you understand that? You've just *got* to."

"Ma'am," said Bill Drake, "ten years ago a man told me I had to go to prison. I broke his head and I left Kansas, and no one has told me what to do since. . . ." He stopped as boots scuffed in the dust behind him and swung around; his hand dropped to his holstered gun.

Andy came out of the circling darkness. Bill stared at him angrily. "I thought I told you to stay with the horses?"

Andy's face was unreadable. "This is your

popular night," he said. "There's a man waiting down on the trail. He wants to talk to you, and he doesn't want to come in to the fire. I think it might pay you to find out what he wants. He thinks he has something interesting to say."

II

Bill Drake looked at his brother for a long moment, trying to read his meaning. Then he glanced at Mary Thorne, catching the sharp curiosity mirrored in the girl's eyes.

"Stay with her," he muttered, and, turning, he vanished toward the trail.

Andy looked after him until he was certain that Bill had gone, then looked back at the girl, his wide mouth twisting a little. "'Tain't often we have this much excitement around our camp, all in one night." He hunkered down on his heels, his back against the spokes of the high wagon wheel, and motioned her toward a nearby rock. "Might as well take it easy. Bill will be gone for a few minutes."

"No."

"You're lucky. Get on your horse, circle around the trail, and ride back to town while you can. Bill's a bad one."

She looked at him, startled. Until that moment she had considered him of no particular importance, thinking that he was merely one of Drake's riders. "That's a strange way to talk about the man you follow."

"He's my brother," said Andy. "I kind of inherited him. I guess maybe I'm no better than he is."

"What would he do if he heard you talking this way?"

"Probably laugh. Us Drakes are great at laughing, even when we're fixing to kill someone."

She flared at him. "Stop talking to me as if I were a child, as if I were someone you could scare. I know when you're joking."

"Sure," said Andy, "I'm joking." He regarded her thoughtfully. She was a spitfire and no mistake. It might be fun to tame her, and from her looks it should be worth the trouble. He said lazily: "Where do you come from, anyway? Haven't you heard the stories they tell about Drake's army? How we burn ranches and blame it on the Apaches? How we murder children and carry off women? You'd better talk to the people in Tucson, or to the colonel at the fort. They'll tell you to stay miles away from Drake's army. Any of them would hang us if they could."

She examined him, noting the bitter lines about his mouth. "I don't believe you're that bad. Your brother just told me that you make your living guarding stagecoaches and ore shipments. Most outlaws would hold them up."

Andy laughed shortly. "And so would Bill if he wasn't being paid to guard them. When they don't pay, we hold them up. We win either way. Everyone's afraid of Bill . . . even his own crew."

"Are you afraid of him?"

Andy thought about it. "I don't know," he said finally. "I've only been out here three months. Ask me after I've been here a year."

She sounded almost peevish. "I wish I knew how much of what you say is true, and how much is kidding. Frankly, if you're trying to scare me, you're wasting your time. I'm perfectly able to protect myself." She let her small hand fall suggestively to the gun at her side.

"Suit yourself." Andy's tone was brusque. He came to his feet in one easy motion. "Stay here. Don't move or you'll be in real trouble." He was gone, fading into the darkness noiselessly before Mary Thorne had a chance to answer.

He moved on feet as silently as an Apache, crossing the broken bottom of the wash to the trail and following it until he was stopped by the low murmur of voices ahead. He crept forward then, using the rocks as shelter, to a point where he could hear everything that was said. The man talking to his brother was the lawyer, Wakeman, and he was arguing heatedly in an undertone.

"I tell you, Bill, this is no wild-goose chase. I remembered the last time that girl's uncle came back to Tucson, and I've checked up on the rest of her story. It's all true. The original party had eleven men and three wagons. They were in the Superstitions all one summer and were headed out when the Indians jumped them. All but two were killed . . . both of them were wounded, but they managed to get back to Tucson, somehow. One of them died a week later. The second, this girl's uncle, had an arrow cut out of his neck, but he pulled through and went home to Texas. Before he left, he sold two nuggets that he'd been carrying in his pocket. They're as big as robin eggs. Silas Martin at the hotel still wears one of them on his watch chain."

Bill Drake still seemed skeptical. "Seems as if the boys . . . having seen all that gold, would have backtracked him?"

"They tried," said Wakeman. "It was only a couple of years after the war. There were few troops in the territory and the Indians were bad. One of the boys got slaughtered and the rest pulled back to town. Twice since, the girl's uncle has come back, but he had no luck. His health was pretty much shot. He wouldn't tell anyone exactly where the lost train was located and they wouldn't take a chance on going with him, blind."

"I don't blame them," said Bill Drake. "These treasure stories are all alike. A lot of men have lost their hair hunting for gold that never existed."

"This exists." The lawyer's voice was harsh

with greed. "Fifty thousand dollars' worth of gold, at least. Think of it, Bill. Fifty thousand dollars can be split between us."

"What about the girl?"

"She's a spitfire," Wakeman said, "but I managed her. I was the first one she talked to when she got to town, and I made certain that she told her story to no one else. Supposing she should disappear. Who would ever guess where she'd gone? Certainly no one would suspect she'd gone with you. This is our chance to get a stake, to get the hell out of this god-forsaken country. Fifty thousand dollars in gold . . ." He rolled the words off his tongue as if he enjoyed uttering them. "Think what you could do with your share."

"I am thinking," said Drake, and there was the note of hidden laughter in his voice. "Are you certain you told no one in Tucson that the girl was riding out to my camp, or that you were coming here tonight?"

"Of course . . . I told no one." Wakeman was impatient. "Do you think I'm a fool?"

"I think maybe you are." Bill Drake had drawn his gun. He fired deliberately, three times.

"A hundred percent is better than half any time, my friend."

Wakeman did not answer. Wakeman was dead. For a long moment Bill Drake stood over the lawyer's body, his heavy gun hanging loosely in his big hand. Then he reholstered it, stooped, caught the dead man under the arms, and dragged his limp body off the trail.

At the sound of the shots the camp exploded with life. Men around the campfire leaped to their feet, calling to each other, calling Bill's name.

Andy glanced quickly around. He had no desire that his brother know that he had been a witness to the murder. He had known that Bill was hard, but he had never seen a man shot down in cold blood before. He ghosted back toward the wash's rim and followed it toward camp, coming down again beyond the chuck wagon.

Mary Thorne was on her feet, staring into the darkness as the crew raced out along the trail. She did not see Andy until he spoke, then swung around, pressing the back of her small hand across her lips.

"Those shots?"

Andy's voice was hoarse. "Remember, I've been with you the full time. I never left you, understand?"

She flushed at his tone, her rising temper fighting with a feeling of nameless panic that was crowding up within her.

"I don't understand. . . ."

He caught her arm. "You don't have to. Just keep quiet and don't ask questions. Come on." He knew Bill would be suspicious unless he showed a natural curiosity.

The girl tried to pull free, but Andy's grip

tightened. He forced her forward, walking at her side, and had scarcely rounded the end of the wagon before they met Bill coming toward them. The rest of the crew was close behind.

"What happened?"

Bill Drake stopped. He looked at Andy, then at the angry girl, and he misunderstood. He grinned at her obvious rage and winked at his brother. "I left you to guard her," he said, "not to manhandle her."

"But the shots?" Mary Thorne still ignored Andy, although he retained his grip on her arm.

"Nothing to worry about." The smile had died from Bill Drake's eyes. "Just a coyote that got too brave." He turned to the cook and his manner became brisk and business-like. "Fetch a lantern. The rest of you bring up the horses and get your duffel loaded."

The crew was used to the swift changes of Bill's mind, but this time he had caught them flat-footed. They started to grumble.

Bill's voice hardened. "We're pulling out. If anyone doesn't like it, he can cut loose and ride on into town."

They hesitated, then slowly turned toward the fire and began to roll the blankets that they had spread only a short hour before.

Bill took the lantern from the cook's hand and led the girl to the far side of the wagon. Ignoring the fact that Andy followed them, he said to

Mary Thorne: "Let's have a look at that treasure map."

"But I thought you . . ."

"Never think," he said. "I've changed my mind. If you have a map a man can read, we'll have a try for your gold."

The girl looked at him, measuring him. "First," she said tensely, "I think we'll talk about how to share it."

"Why sure." Bill Drake was suddenly easy to please. "What would you figure is the proper divvy?"

She considered him, saying slowly: "I'll have to pay Mister Wakeman for his trouble and you'll have to pay your crew. Supposing we split whatever gold we find. You pay your men from your share and I'll take care of Mister Wakeman."

Bill Drake pretended to study the proposition. Watching him, Andy thought that his brother would have made a great actor or a great gambler.

"Why, that sounds fair," Bill said. "Of course, I won't have much for myself once I pay the men and Andy here." He threw a sly glance toward his watching brother. "Andy will want half of everything that I get. It's a deal. Let's have a look at your map."

Mary Thorne drew out the square, folded paper and silently handed it to Bill Drake. She did not glance toward Andy, but Bill motioned his younger brother forward to hold the lantern.

Spreading out the map, Bill studied the wavering lines, grunting to himself as he puzzled out each landmark, tracing over the route with a stubby forefinger.

The girl watched him, making no effort to conceal her eagerness. "Do you think we can find it?"

He looked at her, then back at the paper, finally lifting his eyes again to her face. "Maybe. If I didn't think there was a chance, I wouldn't be trying. Your uncle seems to have known what he was doing, but the country is very rough. Every cañon looks the same. A man can get lost within half a mile of his own camp. It's big, and it's dry, and there's a good chance that we won't come out alive." He folded the paper. "But we'll find it, if it's there to be found." He tapped the folded map with one finger. "This shows where the wagon train was burned, but it tells nothing about the gold. Did they manage to hide it, or was it still in the wagons when the Indians broke through?"

"They hid it," the girl said. "My uncle told me where it is, but I'm not going to tell you now. If I did . . . there would be no need for you to take me along. I don't trust you that far, Bill Drake."

Andy expected his brother to show anger. No one talked to Bill Drake that way, but, instead, his brother was chuckling before she finished.

"I like her," he said to Andy. "You can have your meek, mild females. This one's got fire and fight.

She doesn't trust me and that proves she has good sense."

The girl flushed and her eyes grew dark.

Bill thrust the folded map into the front of his sweat-stained shirt and turned to his brother. "Get your gear together and get her horse. It's time we rolled out." He went around the wagon, leaving Andy and the girl to stare at each other.

Mary Thorne said tartly: "I never met anyone like your brother. One minute he tells me he has no interest in my gold . . . the next he can't even wait until morning before pulling out. I wonder what made him change his mind."

Andy knew why Bill was pulling out so hurriedly. He knew Bill wanted to be well away from Tucson before anyone came looking for Wakeman. Andy's impulse was to tell the girl, to try to get her away from the camp as quickly as he could. But he doubted that she would go without an argument, and, if Bill guessed what he was about, neither of them would ever return to Tucson.

In the short time since he had joined the band, he had noted that there was nothing careless about his brother's lawlessness. Bill seldom left anything to chance. He would have Wakeman's body hidden and he would not leave the girl behind to tell that he had been connected with Wakeman in any way.

Andy was depressed as he turned toward the

horses. Already the crew was saddling. He loaded his gear onto the bay, led the bay back to the chuck wagon, left it with the girl, and went around to get her horse. As he came back, a riderless mount broke out of the bushes and nosed over to the other horses.

Andy heard Mary Thorpe catch her breath, and turned to see her stare at the saddled animal with widening eyes. She came forward slowly, reaching out to touch a dark stain, which smeared across the saddle. She whirled to find Andy watching her, and said in a stifled voice: "Blood. And that's Mister Wakeman's horse. I've seen him ride it. I've . . ." The words caught in her throat. The next instant she seized the reins of her own mount and, swinging up into the saddle, spun it toward the trail.

But quick as she was, Andy was quicker. He caught the bridle before the horse came halfway around and jerked it back. "What do you think you're doing?" he said in a sharp undertone.

She raised her small whip and tried to strike him. "Let me go. I'm riding back to Tucson."

His free hand came up, caught the whip, and wrenched it from her grasp. "You're not going anywhere," he told her. "Not unless you want to get killed. Now stop acting like a fool. And whatever happens, remember you didn't see Wakeman's horse."

He did not wait for her answer, but, sweeping

off his hat, he cut it sharply across the nose of the lawyer's horse. The animal reared, pivoted on its hind hoofs, and dove off into the deep shadows.

For a moment the girl was too startled to speak, then anger flooded through her. "Your brother killed . . ."

"Shut up!" Andy grabbed her arm and pulled her out of the saddle. She clawed at his face. He twisted her arms behind her back.

"You spitfire, behave yourself." He was shaking her. "If you want to live, you know nothing about Wakeman's murder. Understand? Nothing. If Bill even suspects that you've guessed the lawyer is dead, I wouldn't give you a penny for your life."

"I'm not afraid."

He said savagely: "If you think because you're a woman it will protect you, you'd better think again. You're in a spot, sister. I'm putting my neck in a sling, trying to help you, but if you're going to act like a damn' fool, to hell with it." He turned her loose and she stood, breathing heavily. Mary Thorne had never before in her life been manhandled. Her anger against Andy at the instant almost blinded her to anything else. She reached down and half drew her gun, then, meeting his eyes, she let it slide slowly back into the holster. In spite of her fury, she said meekly: "But . . . but what's going to happen?"

"Who knows?" Andy's young face suddenly grew very old in the yellow lantern light. "We'd both better pray that we never find that gold. You'll be fairly safe until then. Bill has very little to do with women as such. He'll probably let you alone, and, as long as he has any use for you, he'll see that the rest of the crew does."

In spite of herself the girl shivered.

"But he won't let you get away. If you try to sneak out, he'll probably have you killed."

She took a deep breath. "But what will happen once we find the gold?"

"I don't know," Andy said. And, turning, he led their horses to the fire.

III

There was little talk as the crew broke camp and headed northward, following roughly the course of the San Pedro. Only the scuff of the horses' hoofs and the *creak* of saddle leather blended with the keening grind from the sun-dried wheels of the chuck wagon. There was almost no talk as the lights of Tucson dropped from sight behind them, masked by a low-lying ridge that paralleled the course they were traveling.

They left the trail and, as far as Mary Thorne could tell, cut out across the desert waste. But Bill Drake, riding at the head of the column, never hesitated.

The spaciousness of the country seemed to

swallow them. The girl was not afraid, having been accustomed to the endless Texas plains. But she was not used to the utter emptiness of this barren land.

The crew rode with watchful caution, men trained to be alert for any danger, knowing that the emptiness, which oppressed the girl, was deceptive. Hostile Indians could be anywhere; even the few whites they might encounter would not be friends.

Bill Drake set the pace and Bill did not hurry. He kept in mind that both men and horses had done thirty miles since the last sunup and that all were tired. They trotted, and walked, and then they dismounted and led their horses; always they kept a packed group with the cook's wagon at their center. To straggle might mean a swift and terrible death.

Mary Thorne rode between the creaking wagon and Andy, at times so close to the younger Drake that her stirrup brushed his in the half darkness. His mere closeness brought a kind of comfort. She was a girl who never before had known fear, a self-reliant girl entirely confident of her own abilities. And she was a little spoiled, in that the men who had come within her circle had always been attracted by her beauty. She had, in fact, a slight contempt for the average man, feeling that she was brighter, shrewder, but she was normally careful to hide these feelings.

But this column of outlaws was something outside her limited experience. It had not occurred to her, when Wakeman suggested that she seek out Bill Drake and his crew, that she could not control them as she had the cowboys who attended the Saturday night dances at the schoolhouse, close to her home ranch.

In Andy she had sensed a difference from the others. His actions in attempting to help her, the light that showed in his eyes when he looked at her would normally have told her that he was attracted to her. But when he had grabbed her and pulled her off the horse, anger stifled her better sense and it took all her effort to control herself.

And she was not quite certain, even now, that all his caution was justified. Even the knowledge that Bill Drake had killed Wakeman could not make her entirely sure. True, she had seen the lawyer's horse with the blood smear across the saddle, but that was not full proof that Wakeman was dead.

Maybe Andy was spooking her. Maybe Andy was attempting to build himself up in her eyes as a protector. Men had done such things before, and, after all, what did she know about either Andy or Bill? Andy had been away when the shots were fired. Perhaps he himself had shot Wakeman and was laying the blame on his older brother.

At the thought, her mouth tightened and her eyes glowed a little. If Andy Drake believed he could make a fool of her, he had better think again. There was not reason for the panic that had been rising in her. She dropped her hand to the small gun at her side and felt its reassuring hardness. *Men,* she thought, *could be controlled, if not by one means, then by others.* She glanced at him, seeing that his eyes were on the trail ahead. She looked, also, through the swirling dust, past the row of intervening riders to where Bill Drake rode alone, big and easy and tireless.

Hard he was, but was he a murderer? Had he killed Wakeman, who seemed to be his friend? If he had, if everything that Andy had hinted at was true, then she was in a serious spot. But she refused to believe it, preferring to trust in her own resources, in her own native ability to pull herself through. She smiled a little then, for the first time since they had begun the long, grim ride. She wished Andy would turn his head, would see the smile, would realize how little she was dependent upon him for aid.

She tried to put him from her mind, but could not. In the east the light was showing faintly, gaining minute by minute, turning the land around them grotesque and unreal and utterly unearthly as it deepened into day. Now she could see the wind-etched banks, the huge piles of rocks that tumbled down the sides of small cañons.

Beside her, Andy rode quietly, solid and real. She glanced again toward him, feeling by instinct that if there were any real safety in the barren land for her, it did lay with Andy. She was drawn toward him, and she fought the feeling, not quite understanding why she fought it. Had he smiled at her then, had he given her any sign of recognition, things might have been different, but he rode with his eyes away from her, ignoring her, as if he were waiting for her to ask for his help.

That, thought Mary Thorne, was something which she would never do. She would ask help from almost anyone except Andy Drake.

It was full dawn before Bill called their halt. He had led them toward the towering mountains and then a short distance into a small cañon. How could he have known there would be a tiny spring? How could he have seen it? It was just a slender trickle of water to be lost in the greedy sands of the dry river course below?

Stiffly the girl lifted herself from the saddle, marveling at the apparent tirelessness of these men. They had ridden all the preceding day, yet few of them showed any real signs of fatigue and they had so schooled their pace that their horses were still not exhausted.

That was the difference between the trained white and the Indian. An Indian would have covered the distance in half the time and killed his horse in the process. The Indian could go on by foot, the white man could not. Drake's crew lived by their horses and with their horses. They came out of the saddle stiffly and coldly and grumpily, silent and morose, yet each man cared for his own mount before he turned back to the chuck wagon where the cook was already doling out the warmed-over beans and the long strips of jerked meat.

Andy offered to care for her horse, but she denied him curtly, rubbing the animal down with handfuls of dry grass, and then carrying her plate from the chuck wagon to a seat that was a little apart from the rest of the camp. The rest of the crew paid her no attention, showing none of the sharp curiosity that had lighted their eyes on the preceding evening.

Even Bill Drake ignored her, sitting by himself on the wagon tongue, his hat shoved far back on his large head, seeming unmindful of the crew, the country, or the morning chill. He ate in silence, and not until he had drained the scalding coffee down to its last muddy dregs and tossed them away did he stir. Then he rose, rolling a cigarette, using a husk in the Mexican fashion. Crossing to the fire, he lifted an ember, holding it lightly between his thumb and forefinger.

At last he turned, facing the crew, and said in an easy voice: "You've all been wondering where we're headed. I'll tell you now. We're going gold hunting." They shifted to watch him. Drake's hard black eyes were as bright as chips of polished lava and they held a spark of mockery as he added: "There won't be any digging, if that's what's worrying you. It was dug twenty years ago by this girl's uncle." He indicated Mary Thorne with a sweeping gesture of his hand, and the mockery reached his lips, curving them. "If you have any ideas about her, forget them. She's a partner . . . nothing more." He waited. The men stared at him. Even the cook had ceased his cleaning up to watch. "She gave me a map," Drake continued. "It shows where her Uncle's party was bushwhacked by Indians. At the time, they were carrying two hundred pounds of gold."

Someone beyond the small fire drew his breath sharply, and Bill Drake's smile widened. "Yes," he repeated, "over two hundred pounds in gold. We're going in after it. We're going to bring it out. And each of you will get a fair share."

Monte Gordon straightened beyond the fire. Monte Gordon was almost as big as Bill Drake. "Going in where?" he asked.

"The Superstitions."

Silence lay for a full moment across the men. Drake broke it. "You aren't afraid to go into the Superstitions, are you, Monte?"

Monte Gordon was big-boned, but his body had been thinned down by much riding and his tissues were dried out from lack of water. His nose had been broken in some forgotten saloon brawl and the last joint of his center finger was missing from his left hand. "I'm not afraid of anything."

94

He was a boastful man. The boastfulness showed in the cant of his shoulders, in the little swagger with which he walked, and in the way his coarse red hair stood almost upright from his round skull. He turned his green eyes toward the girl, looking her over as if he were inspecting a horse. A half-sneering, twisting smile lifted one corner of his thin mouth.

Mary Thorne met the look and felt color rush to her face. She was angry with Drake, but she measured Gordon, studying him, guessing at his weaknesses. If she had to fight for survival with this group of men, she meant to fight as intelligently as she could. Gordon saw her meet his look squarely and misunderstood. His smile widened. Something made the girl glance sideways toward where Andy sat. She found that the younger Drake was watching Gordon without appearing to.

Bill Drake had not taken his attention from Gordon's face. He said, slurring his words a little: "Of course, you aren't afraid of anything, Monte. You're a big, brave, strong man. I've never doubted it. That's the reason I've kept you riding with me."

The crew laughed as Gordon scowled. The laughter put them into better humor, which was what Bill Drake intended. Quick to seize the opportunity, he drew the folded map from his shirt.

"Come and look," he invited. "It's a good map . . .

95

well drawn. And if it's accurate, we should be able to find this cañon." He squatted down and spread it on the ground as they crowded about him. Even the cook deserted the tailboard of the wagon to have his look, but Andy made no motion to join them. He lay four feet from Mary Thorne's elbow, his long legs extended, his body propped half upright against the rock.

She glanced at him again, and there was malice in her tone as she said quietly: "Don't you want to see the map?"

He turned to look at her with a leisureliness that she found irritating. "What for?"

She was angry. "Doesn't gold interest you?"

He sat up, pulling his knees back until he could wrap his long arms around his shins. "Not much."

She was startled, distrusting his words. "But I thought that everyone wanted gold."

"Why?"

"Well, for what it will buy."

Andy Drake looked at her fully then, and his meaning was insultingly clear. "All right, what will it buy?"

Mary Thorne knew exactly what he meant. He was asking her plainly what price she was prepared to pay to get the gold. She pretended to misunderstand. "What does anybody ever want money for?" she said sharply.

"You got me," said Andy. "I never wanted much. I still don't."

She looked at him, feeling savage. "You're making fun of me again."

"Maybe I am," he said, suddenly gentle. "You're very pretty when you get mad."

She flushed. For a moment her guard was down. He could be very attractive, very likeable when he chose.

"And you ruffle your feathers just like a bantam hen my mother used to have. I guess I'll call you Bantam."

She did not like that and said so.

Andy told her seriously: "There'll be a lot of things you won't like before this trip is finished, little Bantam." He had lowered his tone, and he glanced toward the group around the map as if to see whether any of them were listening.

She stared at him, wondering again if she could trust him.

"That's what hunting for gold got you into." There was no amusement in Andy's eyes now. "There's not a man in that bunch who wouldn't slit a throat or shoot his best friend in the back for that much gold. A lot of them have done things for much less, and their records with women aren't good."

"Don't forget that I still have my gun," she said tightly.

He shook his head. "One gun, two guns, even three guns wouldn't do very much good."

She bit her lip. "I've always taken care of

myself in any company. I'll take care of myself here."

"Suit yourself." He was hurt, angry at her rebuke.

"What do you want me to do?"

He had meant to tell her that she could trust him, that whatever happened he would be there to help. Instead, he said: "I don't know." He rose as he spoke. "If I were you, I'd pick myself a man and hang onto him. He'd protect you from the others . . . maybe, if he could."

She stared up at him. "And I suppose you expect me to pick you. That's what you've been working for ever since I came to camp last night. You've been trying to scare me, hoping I'd fall into your arms. Well, I don't fall into any man's arms."

There was just enough truth in what she said to spark Andy's anger. "Suit yourself," he said, "but when you pick a man, pick a strong one." He turned and strode past the group around the fire, leaving the girl alone with her thoughts.

They were far from pleasant. Despite her brave words she was frightened, and yet she could not pull back even if the chance offered.

When the horse had fallen with her father, leaving him a helpless cripple, it had seemed to her that she would have no great trouble in running their Texas ranch. But that was before three years of storms had cut their herd and before the bank loans had come due. This was her last desperate effort to save the ranch, and to raise the money for the operations, which the doctors hoped might straighten her father's back. Only when there had been no other course had she thought of her uncle's tales of the lost wagon train. He had been dead for almost four years and she had not even known exactly where he had hidden the old map. She had searched through the house, finding it finally in the bottom of a cowhide trunk at the rear of the attic.

The treasure had never seemed real to her as a child. It had been one of the fairy stories to which she had listened with the greatest of enjoyment. But looking at the old map and reading again her uncle's letters, it had seemed that all she needed to do was to come to the territory, find the right man, and recover the treasure. She had sent her father to stay with an aunt in Austin, left the ranch in the hands of the foreman, and taken the new railroad to Tucson. Her meeting with Wakeman had been no accident. The lawyer's name had appeared in two of her uncle's letters, and she had gone to his office at once, showing him the map and telling him the full story. It had been Wakeman who had warned her not to tell anyone else in Tucson about the map. The warning had been unnecessary, since there were few people in the small, mud-walled town who she would have thought of taking into her confidence.

Her arrival had created enough stir. There were

few women in the territory and everyone had been helpful. But she had kept her own counsel, and there was certainly nothing that would lead her newfound acquaintances to guess that she had joined Bill Drake, even if anyone in Tucson knew that the outlaw had camped so close to town on the preceding evening.

No one knew where she was. She looked across to where the men were gathered around Drake, staring down at her map, arguing among themselves, and for a moment she felt utter hopelessness. She studied the bearded faces, looking for some hint of kindness, and could find none. Even the bald-headed cook's small eyes glinted with greed, which he made no attempt to hide.

But Andy still showed no interest in the map. He stood hip-shot, his weight resting on his right leg, his shoulders supported by the high wagon side, his thoughtful eyes on the grouped men rather than the map. He was not looking at Mary, but she studied him, remembering with anger his parting words.

Pick yourself a man and let him protect you from the others if he can. That was what he'd told her, and he had acted as if he did not care who she picked. She had no way of knowing that he had hoped she would choose him.

Damn him, she thought. *Damn them all.* She was not the type to go up to a man, hat in hand, and beg his protection. And yet, could she protect herself? She was too smart to think that she could survive alone, and there was merit in what Andy had said.

Bill Drake was the obvious choice. Bill was the strongest man in camp, the one most feared by his companions, the one they were used to obeying. She would have a good chance at personal safety if the outlaws thought she was Bill Drake's woman. But did Bill Drake want her? Andy had said that Bill had very little use for women as such. Of course, she probably could work on him. She was vain enough to believe that her beauty could attract almost any man. But inwardly she shuddered at the idea. Bill Drake was a murderer. The very idea of giving her body to him brought shivers. She felt that as long as she could play with him, promising much yet giving little, she might have a chance to control him. But how long would she be able to manage that?

And once he had taken her, what then? Would he turn away from her, smiling the same little secret smile, unmoved and unaffected, as he had after his murder of Wakeman? No, she could not give herself to Drake. His strength attracted her, but his cold brutality held her away.

Her eyes went around the circle. They stopped at Monte Gordon. Gordon was almost as large as Drake, but a braggart, a man who liked to appear important in his fellows' eyes. Such a man would be far easier to handle. A girl could play on his vanity, win him with praise. But was he strong enough for her purpose, and would she be able to give herself to him? Instinctively she hated him. Instinctively she knew that, with all his boasting, Monte Gordon would back down when it came to a fight with the whole crew. She needed someone stronger than Gordon—stronger than the whole crew.

In fact, she needed the whole crew. The frown, which had drawn a small crease between her eyebrows, eased and a tiny smile touched her lips. *That was it, the whole crew. Why not promise each man something when the hunt was done, make each man believe that he alone had a claim upon her after the gold was found? Why not play them all, one against the next, promising everything, giving nothing in return?*

The thought brought a slight flush to her cheeks. She had known women who made their livings in that way, who promised much and gave little. She had despised them. But in the situation she faced, there was no room for niceties and conventions played no part. Her future was bound to this crew of outlaws, these murderers. If she hoped to live, she must fight with any weapon that was offered, at least until the gold was found. She was, she thought, fairly safe until that time. Bill Drake needed her for that long. It was afterward that counted, after the treasure was located.

If she could make friends with the crew by that

102

time, they might well stand with her against Drake. She did not know what plans Drake had for her. She was almost certain that he did now know that she had seen Wakeman's horse with the telltale stain of blood on the saddle, but she could not be certain.

Bill Drake was not as easy to read as were some of the others. Drake kept his own thoughts to himself and he had shown no sign of being impressed by her beauty. That beauty must be her main weapon. She had used it before, flirting with the riders and small ranchers at the school dances, testing her power over them as any girl would, but not doing it with any real purpose. They had all wanted her, but she had never given into any of them. But if she could attract the riders around the ranch, she certainly could attract these women-starved outlaws. If only one of the crew wanted her, she would be in serious danger. If two were filled with desire, they might fight over her, and the winner claim his reward, but if all fifteen were fascinated, then each would help keep the others within proper bounds.

Her natural confidence that had been wearing thin through the long dark hours of the ride returned and she straightened a little, ready now to face the future, certain that she could out-think and out-guess these men who threatened her.

Her eyes strayed to Andy and gained a certain bitterness. Of all the crew, he was the only one who attracted her. If he had offered to help, if he had tried to get her away from the camp, none of this would be necessary. It was, she thought, partly his fault. She would punish him, using him as she planned to use the others, and then giving nothing in return. *I'll show him,* she thought. *Let him watch. I'll give him plenty to watch. Then we'll see how he likes it.*

She rose, throwing a smile at the gathered men. None of them raised their heads. The smile was mocking. It was the same smile with which she had turned aside the advances of her father's riders, but now it had gained a quality of deadliness, which it had never had before. She was like a beautiful cat, surrounded by a pack of snarling dogs. She gathered up her blankets, crossed to a shadow thrown by a huge rock, and arranged them on the hard ground. Then she went to sleep.

IV

Monte Gordon was serving as horse guard. Never a man to exert himself when motion was unnecessary, he sat with his back against a boulder, rifle across his outstretched knees, hat drawn low to keep the hot afternoon sun from his eyes.

The camp slept. The horses drowsed, finding

what little shade they could from the brush and overhanging rocks. Heat waves came up from the scorched earth to eddy in the motionless air, hanging above the cañon floor like layers of almost translucent smoke.

Gordon yawned, squinting his green eyes against the glare. He looked older than his twenty-seven years. His fair skin had been roughened and reddened by constant burning until its hue suggested the shell of an overdone lobster. His mouth was thin-lipped, cruel. The deep creases, which ran up from the mouth's corners toward his nose, gave his narrow face a pinched look. His beard was thin, and against the darkened skin the quarter-inch whitish stubble hardly showed.

He heard a sound and was at once alert, his powerful hands grasping the hot barrel of the rifle. His apparent lassitude dropped away from him like a cloak. He was a man who could move quickly and sharply on occasion, and he brought the gun around in a half arc before he saw the girl. He watched her, a slow grin spreading his thin lips so that his stained teeth showed. But the grin did not reach his eyes. They remained cold and calculating and alert as Mary Thorne moved up the uneven path toward where he sat.

She had been to the spring and had rinsed her face and hands and she managed to look clean and fresh, despite the heat and the dust and the fact that she had slept on the ground. "The rest are sleeping," she said as she reached Gordon's side and stood above him, smiling down at him. "But it's hot . . . far too hot to sleep."

His eyes measured her, shamelessly taking in every curve of her lithe body and liking what they saw. His mouth quirked at the corners. Monte Gordon had a very good opinion of himself. He considered that he was as fast with a gun as any man in the territory. He had killed three times, not counting Mexicans, and had built himself a reputation for senseless cruelty. He also prided himself in his conquests with women. It did not surprise him that this girl would seek his company.

"Sit down." He motioned to a place that was partly in shade. "This is a bad country for a woman."

"A bad country for anyone," she agreed as she settled herself at his side.

His voice was eager. "Tell me about the gold. It is really there? You're sure there was as much as your uncle said? Did he know what he was doing when he drew that map?"

She nodded. "He told me all about it when I was a little girl. It was placer gold, and coarse. They found it high up on the cañon side, in an old watercourse, but there was no water there then. They worked it dry, tossing it in the air with a blanket so that the wind blew the dust away and left the nuggets. They worked hard all summer, and they were coming out when they were attacked. You don't need to worry. The gold is there. Show me where the wagon train was burned, and I'll take you to the rock crevice where they hid the gold. The problem is, can we get to it and can we get it out? Will the Indians leave us alone?"

Monte Gordon could not help boasting. "The Apaches are afraid of us. Everyone in the territory is afraid of us . . . even the yellowlegs from the forts."

"They're afraid of Bill Drake," she corrected him. "They aren't afraid of you or me."

The corners of Monte Gordon's mouth turned down sharply. "Where would Bill Drake be if it wasn't for the men who ride with him? He couldn't fight the Indians alone and he couldn't keep the soldiers off his neck. He's only one man, remember."

"But what a man." Bitterness crept into her tone and she stared off across the broken land, apparently paying no attention to Gordon. "Everyone's afraid of him, and I don't blame them. I'm scared, too."

"I'm not." As soon as the words had left his lips, Monte Gordon glanced instinctively around to see if anyone could have overheard. The motion was involuntary. He would not admit even to himself that he feared Bill Drake, but even so he wanted to be certain that his words would not be carried back to Drake. Nothing in the camp below them stirred. Reassured, he looked again at the girl, then had a momentary doubt, wondering if she would repeat what he had said.

Studying her, he could not make up his mind. She was something new in his experience. She was not like the girls he had known in the railroad towns in Kansas, or the women who lived in the back alleys of Tombstone and the newer mining camps. She simply did not fit into his mental picture at all. She had no business riding across this waste, camping on the ground, sharing meager food with outlaws, uncomplainingly taking what came along the trail. His voice was suddenly harsh.

"What do you want?"

"Want?" Mary Thorne's eyes widened. "I want the gold my uncle dug. I want it so badly that I've come a thousand miles . . . so badly that I'd take it at the point of a gun. But now I'm afraid that once I get it, it will be taken away from me."

Monte Gordon was not a quick thinker. He turned her words over in his mind, searching them for a possible hidden meaning. "You don't mean the Indians. I told you that the Indians would leave us alone."

"I don't mean the Indians."

"Nor the Army?"

"Nor the Army." Mary Thorne was seized with a sudden impulse to laugh at him, to grab his shoulders and shake him. She had not, she thought, realized how stupid Monte Gordon could be.

"Then who are you afraid of?"

It was her turn to glance across her shoulder. She would not have been surprised had she found Bill Drake's powerful figure standing behind her, grinning down at her with that mocking look in his eyes that she had learned to hate and fear. For much as she fought against it, her fear of the elder Drake was a real, a poignant thing. She could not rid herself of it. But the camp below was still quiet. Apparently everyone was still asleep. She looked around at the barren, empty land, then back at Gordon.

"A lawyer sent me out to see Bill Drake last night," she said in a controlled undertone. "A man named Wakeman."

Monte Gordon had known Wakeman. His interest, previously dulled by the heat, stirred and sharpened and came alive.

"Yes?"

Mary Thorne threw everything into the gamble. "Bill Drake murdered Wakeman last night on the trail below your camp. Those were the shots you heard."

Monte Gordon knew this, also. One of the men who had been detailed to dispose of Wakeman's body was a friend. But he held his comment, merely nodding.

Mary Thorne felt disappointment at his lack of

surprise. She had thought her words would jar him. She steadied her voice and went on, sounding a trifle breathless.

"With Wakeman dead, no one in Tucson knows where I am. No one knows I rode out with Drake. When the gold is found, what's to prevent Bill Drake from doing away with me?"

Monte Gordon found this amusing. To him murder was a simple everyday act. A man was in your way and you killed him. But Monte Gordon had never yet had occasion to kill a woman, and he grinned. "Shame to do away with a girl as pretty as you are."

Mary Thorne knew that she flushed, and she did not meet his eyes as she said: "Bill Drake doesn't care anything about that. All he's interested in is the gold."

Gordon nodded slowly. Bill Drake's lack of interest in women had always puzzled the crew, and Gordon accepted her words without argument. "So what is it you want of me?" He repeated the question.

For a moment she was entirely honest. "I want to live."

His grin widened.

"And I want my gold, too."

He could understand that.

"And I have to have someone who will protect me."

A small bell of warning sounded in Monte

Gordon's dull brain. This girl had come seeking him because she wanted someone to protect her, to protect her from Bill Drake. This called for careful thought. She was very desirable. He had never in his wild years met anyone who struck him as half so desirable, and he could imagine himself standing up to Bill Drake in a fight. He might even brag about his intention—but when it came to a showdown, could he move faster than Drake? Had he any real chance of killing the outlaw leader?

Mary Thorne saw his hesitation and guessed its cause. "You've had a look at the map," she said quickly. "You know it shows where the wagons were attacked, but that it doesn't show where the gold was buried. No one, except I, knows where the gold is. Unless I choose to tell, Bill Drake will never find it. No one can find it. That is one of the things I have to trade." She looked deeply in his eyes as she said it. She hoped desperately that her slight shudder of revulsion was not noticeable to the red-haired man. She thought: *Dear God, give me the strength to go through with this. Make me strong enough, certain enough to beat these hoodlums at their own game. . . .*

"Bill will make you tell," Gordon said.

She nodded. "He will unless you and your friends are on my side, unless we stand together against him. Whether you want to help me or not, it's in your interest to stand against Drake. If he would kill Wakeman to get the lawyer's share, he certainly would not hesitate to kill me to get mine. And it's entirely possible that he might want to be rid of the rest of his crew so that he won't be called upon to split with you."

"He needs us." Gordon sounded confident. "He couldn't carry on in the territory without us. Unless he has the crew at his back, he's just another brush-jumper dodging the law."

"That's true." She nodded again. "He does need you if he means to keep on doing business in this country. But what if he should manage to get all that gold for himself? Would he need you or anyone then? With that much gold, you certainly don't believe that he would linger in this wilderness. He'd pull out, and he'd leave the crew to whistle for themselves."

This was a new thought. She almost smiled as she watched Gordon consider it, and saw by the change in his eyes that he believed this was exactly what Drake meant to do. *I've got him,* she thought. *He's mine if I play my cards carefully.*

Monte Gordon had never been loyal to anyone in his life. It was not at all difficult for him to believe that Bill Drake meant to take the gold and desert the crew. Had their positions been reversed, that was exactly what he would have attempted. But he still argued with the girl.

"You don't know for sure that's what he plans."

"No," she admitted. "I don't know, but I have a

feeling. I don't want to be killed. I don't want to be deserted, and I don't want to lose my share of the treasure. And if you would stand with me, we could make certain that it would not happen."

He was wavering. "There's not a great deal we can do alone."

"No." Her smile was warm now for she knew that she had won. "We can't do much alone, but you have friends among the men . . . friends who hate Bill Drake as you do, friends who would stand with you if they thought they could share the gold."

"And afterwards . . . ?" He reached out a hand, laying it on her arm, his questing eyes taking in the proud rise of her breasts, the warm symmetry of her lithe body.

She met the look without flinching. "Afterward, when it's safe, we can go to my ranch."

Monte Gordon's pale eyes burned. He was certain now of his conquest, too vain to doubt but that the girl was as attracted to him as he was to her. He leaned forward, meaning to kiss her, but she held him away.

"Not here. If Bill Drake should see us, everything would be endangered. We must wait."

He was sulky under her refusal, but she was confident now. She told him steadily: "Listen, Monte. Why do you think I chose you? Because you're the really solid man of the crew, and the smartest. We've got to play our cards carefully.

We aren't ready yet for a showdown. We've got to wait until we find the place where the wagon train was burned. Until that time we need Drake and the rest of the crew. If we don't have them, we'll stand no chance against the Indians."

He nodded slowly, agreeing.

"But once we reach the wagon train, once we know where the gold is hidden, then we'll have to strike and strike fast. We've got to be ready for that moment. You've got to enlist all the help you can. You've got to talk them over to our side and you've got to let me talk with them."

Monte Gordon felt a genuine flash of admiration for this girl. He sensed that she could hold her own with any man. He grinned. "There's not one of them that can resist you, lady, but don't promise them too much."

She matched his grin. "Don't worry about me Monte. Together we're unbeatable. But if you see me talking to any of the men, don't get angry. What promises I make will be made for one reason only . . . to get them to stand against Bill Drake . . . and those promises will not be kept."

He laughed outright, extending his hand. She took it gravely, not guessing his intent, and felt herself pulled roughly against him. She felt the pressure of his mouth against hers and started to struggle. Then she forced herself to lie quietly in his arms. His kiss was long and hungry. It burned against her lips. He freed one hand and slid it around her neck, under the protecting scarf and down under her shirt until it cupped about one of the proud young breasts.

"By God!" Monte Gordon's breath came shortly, his red-rimmed eyes showed flame. "By God . . ." He kissed her again.

"Please," she said. "Careful, you'll ruin everything." She pushed herself away from him, rearranging her clothes. She managed a smile then, although never afterward did she remember how she managed it.

"By God," he said, and laughed. "By God, I can wait. A thing like you is well worth waiting for."

V

Andy Drake watched Mary Thorne return to camp. He had been awake for half an hour and he had seen her up the hill with Monte Gordon. But he lay perfectly quiet, his hat shading his face, so that it was impossible to tell whether he was asleep or awake.

He had seen her when she first stirred on her blanket, watched her as she bathed her face at the creek, and then observed her walking out to Monte Gordon's post. The rocks had partly screened his view of the meeting, but he had seen enough. He felt like killing Gordon.

Lying there he thought: *She's no damn' good. I*

felt sorry for her, and she immediately plays up to Gordon. Andy Drake had had little experience with women. He did not realize that he was in love. He knew only that he was hurt and resentful, and filled with a desire to hurt others. But he waited until the other members of the crew stirred. He rose, still deeply troubled, moved down to the thread-like stream, and bathed his face and arms in the tepid water.

The heat of the late afternoon pushed down upon him with the force of a blast from a smoking furnace. He came back to the circle of the camp and stopped to watch the cook who already was busy at the tailboard of the wagon. Then he moved on out to help bring in the horses and water them at the small hollow that had been scooped out below the spring.

After they had eaten and the two casks and the canteens had been filled, they lifted themselves stiffly into the saddles and headed northwest-ward toward where the mountains rose, purple-shadowed and mysterious in the last rays of the setting sun.

Andy was riding at the head of the column, close to his brother's side, a good fifty feet in advance of the main body of the crew. The Drakes rode in silence for a good three miles, not forcing the horses, letting them pick their pace and path.

"I see," Bill Drake said finally, "that Monte Gordon is showing interest in your girl."

Andy flinched. He hesitated for an instant before turning to look at his brother. It was the first time Bill had spoken since they had broken camp. He took his time to school his voice before he answered.

"I don't know what you are talking about."

Bill Drake grinned to himself, and, when he spoke, it was as if he were addressing himself rather than Andy. "A man," he said, "always turns secretive when he begins to get interested in a woman. I watched you this afternoon. You pretended to be asleep, but you were awake when she went down to the stream, awake when she moved out to talk to Gordon."

Andy found it difficult to speak. He had not guessed that Bill, too, was awake. "You told me last night that I should mind my own business," he said sullenly. "That goes both ways."

"I'm minding my business," Bill told him. "A woman thrown in with a bunch of men is like a keg of dynamite. She can have a worse effect than all the gold that will ever be dug in these mountains. Her very existence will cause quarrels and jealousies."

Andy scowled. "It was you who decided to go on this fool gold hunt . . . you who brought her along. You should have refused to listen last night. You should have sent her back to Tucson."

Bill looked at him. "What about the gold?"

"What about it?" said Andy. He felt trapped.

117

In spite of his anger against the girl, he had to protect her, somehow, from Bill. He knew Bill would never let her go back to Tucson, now that Wakeman was murdered.

Wakeman for all his faults had occupied a certain place in the territory and his murder might well bring down the wrath of the military on Bill's head. Bill understood this as well, if not better than Andy, and the younger Drake was caught between a certain loyalty to Bill, a fear for the girl, and his anger against her. He said now unwillingly: "What do you mean to do with her, Bill? I mean, after the gold is found?"

Bill shrugged. "That's one thing I haven't decided."

Andy surprised himself by saying: "Play fair. Give her a fair share of the gold. Let her go back where she came from."

"What makes you think that I mean to do anything else?"

Andy hesitated. He realized that he could not explain what he meant without admitting to his brother that both he and Mary Thorne knew of Wakeman's murder. He said harshly, trying to carry it off: "Because I've watched you for the last few months. What you do you do for Bill Drake and no one else."

His older brother was genuinely surprised. "And who else would I be doing it for? Listen, kid, you're young. You've had no experience and you're soft. There's no place out here for a soft man. You'll have to get that through your head or you won't live long. If I thought you were going soft on me, I'd send you riding out of here this afternoon."

Andy shut his lips. It was fruitless to argue. There was an unreal quality in the whole conversation, in the whole situation. A year before, he could not have pictured himself riding across this waste with a crowd of outlaws. He stared at his horse's ears, realizing how very little he actually knew about Bill. There was a ten-year difference in their ages, and Bill had been gone from home almost before Andy's first memory. Only chance had thrown them together again when Bill recognized the family resemblance and asked him his name on the street in Tombstone.

And in the three months since he had first ridden with the crew, Bill had seldom spoken of himself, of his experiences or of his desires. He had in effect held Andy at arm's length, treating him as he treated any of the other riders, keeping his own counsel and showing no curiosity about his brother. This was the first time they had really talked together and the gulf of misunderstanding, which separated their points of view, loomed wider than Andy had imagined.

Bill endured his silence for half a mile. Then he said: "I want an understanding with you now. There's a showdown coming. I can feel it. I can smell it in the air. The girl is going to cause trouble. She's going to tear this crew apart and turn it into a bunch of snarling, snapping dogs. Where do you stand when that happens? Are you with me, or has she gotten to you?"

Andy did not answer.

"Let me warn you," said his brother. "I know a hell of a lot more about women than you ever will. That's why I let them alone, mostly. That girl is a spitfire. She knows she's pretty. She's no tramp, but she still knows what effect she can have upon a man. She's not one of these wishy-washy females that get dressed up in silks and laces and faint every time a man frowns at her. She can fight, and, when she fights, she can be as deadly as a rattlesnake."

"And what does this have to do with me?"

"I don't know," Bill said. "Frankly your tongue is hanging out at the sight of her even though you don't show it as plainly as that fool Gordon. Watch your step. Put her out of your mind, if you can. I wish I thought you could. I wish we'd never seen her. I've got a hunch about her. I've got a hunch that the worst mistake I ever made was when I decided to go after that gold. But the cards are on the table and the hand's dealt. The only thing we can do is to choose out sides and carry on the best we can." He grinned suddenly. "Make up your mind. You're either with me or against me. There isn't any place for you in between."

VI

The bald-headed cook was named Frank Page, but it had been so long since anyone had called him by his right name that he had almost forgotten it. He had been cooking for a mine crew down below the border when he had a run-in with the foreman and killed the man with a singlejack.

The foreman had been popular and the cook had had to run for his life. He had headed into the wild mountains with no real hope of ever getting back to the American side. The mountains were filled with Mexican renegades, bronco Indians, and wild animals. He had been unarmed, and, if he did not fall prey to some of the outlaws, there was a better than even chance that he would starve.

He had nearly starved, for by the time Bill Drake's men stumbled across his camp, he was too weak to run. Most of the crew had been for letting him die, figuring that a man so old and feeble would be worse than useless. But Bill Drake had been in one of his humorous moods and it amused him to question the ragged scarecrow.

"What can you do, pop?"

Page had glared at him, his old eyes so sunken in his thin face that they were hard to see. "I can cook." He had been past caring what they did with him. At first, he had assumed that they were a

121

posse of the foreman's friends, come out from the mine to hang him.

"Why," Bill Drake had said, and chuckled to himself, "we need a cook. There isn't a bunch of brush-jumpers in the territory that can boast a chuck wagon. We'll get us a wagon and we'll have warm victuals. And maybe we'll take some of the wrinkles out of our bellies."

He had laughed, and the old man, thinking Bill was making fun of him, had tried to throw a rock. But Drake had taken him north of the line. He'd bought a wagon and stocked it and they had hauled it over some of the roughest country that a wagon had ever traversed, at times forced to use a dozen saddle lines to help the struggling team. The wagon was almost as famous in the country as Drake's army, and none was prouder of it than Frank Page. He felt that it was his, and he never allowed one of the other men to crawl under the canvas-covered bows. It was his home, his castle, and he would have killed to protect it.

But past midnight the old cook noticed that Mary Thorne was drooping in her saddle from sheer weariness. He had watched her since she had first come into the camp, feeling a faint stirring in the old dried-up lump, which was his heart. Somewhere he had a daughter. He had not seen her in fifty years, but, in his mind's eye, he pictured her as a young woman, perhaps resembling Mary Thorne.

They halted at one o'clock, and, while they rested, breathing the horses, he sidled over to where the girl sat listlessly, her eyes closed, her head drooping forward in half sleep. "There's room on the wagon seat," he said, "and it's easier than the saddle. You can curl up and sleep."

Mary Thorne opened her dark eyes and peered up at him. She saw nothing reassuring. He was old, dried out, and dirty, a little man with bandy legs and a ring of brownish-white hair that circled a shining scalp. His eyes were blue, but his squint was so tight that it was difficult to see the pupils.

"Why, thank you," she said, and, when Bill Drake gave the word to move out, she was perched on the high seat at the cook's side, a blanket folded around her against the night's chill, her horse tied to the tailgate.

"It's a rough country," said the cook. His pipe was short and black and smelled vilely of cheap tobacco. "Only an idiot would ever come to it."

"There's the gold," she said, and studied him, trying to read his thoughts. "What do you plan to do with your share of the gold?"

New life came into the cook's voice. What would he do with his share of the wagon train gold? A whole panorama of dreams opened up to fill his old mind. "Why," he said slowly, "I guess I'll go back."

"Back where?"

"To New York state. It's got grass and trees and

123

water aplenty. I'll go back and build me a house by a stream I know and listen to the water as it runs." He fell silent, thinking of the water until he could almost hear the sound of it gurgling as it coursed down over the boulders. Water—what a wonderful thing water was. A man never realized how important it was until he came out into a dry country. And then his dream faded slowly and reality returned. He heard the *creak* of the wagon, the grind of the iron tires over the lava rock, splintered and rough and sharp with the edge of a thousand knives.

He knew that, no matter how much gold he found, he would never get back to the East. He had made strikes before and the money had lasted only until he hit a town, only until he had reached the first saloon that boasted a poker game or a faro bank. For the cook was a gambler. He had been a gambler all his life—not the kind of gambler who made a living at cards, but a man obsessed with the desire to play. It was worse than drink, far worse than the hunger for women. It tore a man inside out and left him broke and disillusioned and hopeless.

A dozen times he had sworn off and as many times he had lasted only until there was money in his pocket again. He gripped the smooth leather of the lines with his knob-knuckled, twisted hands and stared out across the rising swell of the rough country ahead, silvered now by the full light of the distant moon, and thought bitterly that it would be far better for him if he had never heard of gold, if they never found the lost treasure for which they were seeking. He turned and looked at the girl, judging her out of his self-bitterness, and he raised his voice so that it carried above the sharp grind of the ungreased wagon wheels.

"Money's a bad thing," he said. "Men fight for it and kill for it and die for it, and after they get it into their hands, what good does it ever do them? You lose it at the first gambling table . . . or drink it up over the first bar. Why does a nice clean girl like you want gold?"

She turned her head. She started to tell him that she needed it to save the ranch, to pay her father's doctor bills, and then she checked herself. What good did it do to explain? What difference could it make if this funny little old man understood? She said tensely: "I want it. Isn't that enough?"

His laughter had a cackling sound that held little mirth. "The world," he told her, "is full of people who want things. It's this want that sends men to the mountains, into the deserts, and at times to hell itself, and they almost never find what they're looking for. They don't find it because they don't have a clear picture of what it takes to make them happy. I had a wife and a girl and a nice farm, but I wanted gold. I went to California, and then to Mexico, and then here. I've found gold, and, if I was strong enough minded,

I'd go back and buy the farm I had once and lost through my own foolishness. So why don't you forget this gold? Go back where you came from while you're still young, while you still have looks. You don't belong in this country. No woman who wants to keep being a woman belongs here. Get out while you can, before it's too late."

"But I can't go." She spoke without thinking. "Bill Drake wouldn't let me go if I wanted to."

The cook squinted at her in the darkness. To him, Bill Drake was one of the greatest men in the world. Of all the assorted crew who rode behind the outlaw he had the deepest feeling of loyalty. Drake had picked him up when he was starving. Drake had gotten him the chuck wagon and prevented the other outlaws from hazing him. Drake had made him feel useful and important just when he had begun to believe that his life was finished. In his simple code that was enough to make him Drake's man for the rest of his time on earth.

"You don't know Bill Drake," he told Mary Thorne. "A lot of men who call Bill names aren't fit to clean his boots. He's one of the most honest people alive."

Mary Thorne was genuinely shocked. She recognized the note of simple loyalty in the cook's voice and realized that she would have to be careful, but her feeling against Drake rode down her natural caution. "You don't know what you're talking about. The man is a cold-blooded murderer. Why . . . why he killed Mister Wakeman last night . . ." As soon as the words were out, she bit her lip, fearful that the cook would carry what she had said back to Drake.

But the cook was not even surprised. From the moment he joined the crew, he had made it a practice to know everything that went on around the camp. And he had Drake's full trust. It had been the cook, in fact, who had helped bury the lawyer's body, heaping stones up on the grave so that no coyote could possibly unearth it. He had felt no shock at Wakeman's death, and no curiosity. Since Bill Drake had done the shooting, he was certain that the lawyer deserved what he got.

"Wakeman was a dog," he said. "Wakeman would have robbed his own grandmother. Why should you be concerned that he's dead?"

The words scared Mary Thorne. She'd had no intention of letting the cook know she even suspected Drake of Wakeman's murder. Her words had burst out in anger. She had always spoken her full mind and it was hard to curb herself, even here. She looked at him and found nothing hostile in his face.

"You may be right," she said in a small voice. "I was angry and shocked. You . . . you won't tell Drake that I said anything, that I even know anything about it?"

The cook was surprised. "Tell who? Oh, Bill. Shucks, I'm not going to tell anyone. But you're worrying about nothing. Bill wouldn't care that you know."

"He would," she insisted. "He'd kill me to keep me quiet. I know he would. Please promise not to tell."

The cook grinned. The idea that one more murder would in any way worry Drake was beyond his comprehension. To his simple mind, Drake was above the law. "You're crazy," he told the girl. "I never even heard of Bill Drake's killing a woman, but, if it will make you easier, I won't tell him. A man gets further in this life if he don't go around repeating all he hears."

VII

In every crew there is a "Kid", and Bill Drake's outfit was no different from the rest. Sometimes the nickname is used for the youngest rider in the crowd, at others it is held by a man who has possessed it from his youth.

The Pecos Kid was young, twenty-one or -two. He did now know exactly how old he was. His mother had been an Army washerwoman. The Kid had never known the name of his father and was not at all certain that his mother had known. He had been born at Fort Smith on the Arkansas and

had run away at nine, drifting West during troubled period following the Civil War.

Where he had picked up his nickname only knew and he had never troubled to tell. He w narrow-faced, tight-lipped, looking a good t years older than his actual age. His body was thi wiry, yet he had the resilience of rawhide and h never seemed to tire.

He rode easily at Monte Gordon's side, rod steadily without speaking as the night lightened and turned gradually into a bright dawn. Gordon studied him from the corner of his eye. All during the ride he had been considering the Kid, for his shifty mind was already laying its plans. These plans were a direct result of his talk with Mary Thorne. Try as he might, he could not get the girl out of his mind.

The very remembrance of her mouth, of her skin, warm under his sweaty hands, turned his thoughts on fire. He wanted her, but he wanted fa more than the girl. He wanted the gold, and h wanted to settle things with Bill Drake. But I was still afraid of Drake. He knew he could n carry out any plan without help, and the Kid w strongest and by far the most dangerous meml of the crew. If he meant to stand against Drake would need the Pecos Kid at his side.

"Long ride," Gordon said, and stretched hin in the saddle as the light finally came acros badlands to the east.

The Kid glanced at him, and then away. His slight body was so thin that it did not look strong enough to support the weight of the two heavy guns that he wore, low-slung and tied down against his flat thighs.

"And for what?" The Kid's words had a certain bitterness.

"For gold," said Gordon, and forced himself to laugh. "You don't mean to tell me you have no interest in gold?"

The Pecos Kid spat in the reddish dust. "I like gold as well as the next." His voice was a rasping whine. "But, hell, who knows whether we'll find any gold at the end of his fool trip? Who knows that fool girl didn't draw the map herself?"

"Why should she?"

"Why's a woman do anything?" The Kid was very bitter about women. A girl in El Paso del Norte had turned him over to the sheriff and he had not trusted women since.

Gordon knew the story. He laughed, then sobered. "The gold will be there, all right. Bill Drake's no fool. He killed that lawyer so he wouldn't have to split it. He wouldn't be riding out here unless he felt sure."

The Kid grumbled. "He may not be a fool but sometimes he acts like one. Other times he acts like God. What are we, his slaves? We ride the brush for weeks . . . and the first night we're within striking distance of a town, he keeps us in camp."

Gordon nodded his agreement. He knew the Kid had felt the rough edge of Drake's tongue more than once, and the Kid was proud. He hated to take orders from any man.

"Drake sets himself pretty high," Gordon admitted.

"He's not so big." The Kid kept nursing his real and fancied wrongs. "A rifle bullet would knock him out of that saddle. The next time he lights into me, he'd better look out for himself."

"Why wait until he lights into you?" Gordon's tone was idle, but the Pecos Kid turned to look at him sharply. His eyes changed as he studied Gordon's bland expression.

"What are you trying to get at?" His eyes probed at Gordon, cold and blue and so light that it was hard to distinguish the pupils. This gave him a peculiar expression, as if his head were only an empty skull, with vacant eye sockets staring out at a hostile world.

Gordon lost his blandness under the look, shivered, and turned his eyes away. "There's supposed to be two hundred pounds of gold," he said, not answering the question directly. "How much of it do you think we'll ever see?"

"We'll see our share."

"Will we?"

"We'd better," said the Kid, and let his left hand drop to the butt of his gun. "There'll be trouble if we don't. Bill Drake has hurrahed us and starved us and ridden us to skin and bones, but he ain't never robbed us, and he knows better than try."

"Does he?" said Gordon. "He killed the lawyer because he wanted half. There are fifteen of us counting the cook. Bill Drake won't be likely to split that gold fifteen ways."

The Pecos Kid thought this over slowly. "So?"

"And you know Drake didn't kill Wakeman without doing some figuring. Wakeman's been handy for us. He dug up a lot of business and managed to sell some of the stuff we picked up along the way. It looks to me like Drake's planning to pull out and take most of the gold with him."

"Maybe."

"So why should we wait for him to make the first move? If he can pull out, why can't we? We can take over when he isn't expecting it. Burns will do what I say. Snyder and Tex Hart will go along. That makes five of us. Five working together with a plan should be enough."

"But we don't know where the gold is."

Gordon's laugh was easy. "No, we don't know where the gold is, and neither does Drake. But the girl does, and she'll side with us. She's a friend of mine and she's afraid of Drake."

The Kid ran the tip of his tongue over his dust-covered lips. "A friend of yours?"

Gordon's laugh became a trifle self-conscious. "I've got a way with women, Kid."

The Pecos Kid looked at him. "You think you have a way with women?"

"Well, I have," said Gordon, and sounded almost hurt. "I didn't even make a play for her. She came to me. I tell you she's afraid of Drake. She'll do almost anything to escape from Drake."

"Oh, she will?" said the Kid. "And who gets her after we find the gold?"

Gordon already had his own plans for Mary Thorne, but he needed the Kid. The point was to string Pecos along, so he said lightly: "Take it easy, Kid. There's a lot of women in the world, but damn' little gold. I'll do anything you say. I'll even cut cards for her, and may the best man win."

"All right." The Pecos Kid had already decided. "You can count me in. But no tricks, or I'll take you to pieces."

"No tricks," Gordon said. He was more than satisfied as he reined his horse back until Tex Hart and Butch Snyder pulled abreast. They were as near real friends as any he had within the crew.

Hart was big, broad of shoulder, and almost middle-aged. Gossip said he had been an officer in the Confederate Army, but Gordon knew that was not true. What little fighting Hart had seen was in guerilla raids along the Missouri border, from where he had fled to Kansas and then to Texas.

Butch Snyder was a little man. No one knew what he had done or where he had come from before he arrived in the territory.

133

With them, Gordon was more open than he had been with the Kid. He outlined his plans in great detail and ended: "Bill Drake thinks he's top man, but, if it wasn't for the rest of us, where would he be?" Neither troubled to answer, so he went on, telling them of the girl's fear of Drake, and of his certainty that they would never receive a fair share of the gold.

"The Pecos Kid is with us," he added, "and, if any man in the bunch can match Bill Drake with a six-gun, it's the Kid."

"And what if Drake kills the Kid?" Tex Hart asked.

"So he kills him." Gordon's voice was filled with indifference. "We'll fix things up so the Kid braces Drake. If Drake goes down, we'll take over. Sticking together, we can handle the rest of the bunch."

"What about Drake's kid brother?"

Gordon looked ahead toward where Andy was still riding at the head of the column. "I'll take care of him myself," Gordon promised. "I don't like him anyhow."

They nodded and rode ahead in silence, each man wrapped deeply in his own thoughts. Before them, some sixty miles distant, the summit of the range rose and took shape in the soft, early morning light. Somewhere in one of the stony, rugged cañons that ran up its sides like lacing fingers, there lay the remains of the burned wagon train, and the wealth in gold for which they all yearned.

At this distance there was nothing mysterious about the rising peaks, nothing at all frightening to these men who were accustomed to barren wilderness. It was just another upthrust, another ridge of mountains in the endless procession of peaks that marched across this dreary land.

They rode onward steadily, wearily, yet at a pace that did not beat out their horses. It was almost ten o'clock before Bill Drake raised his hand, and the cook swung the chuck wagon into the mouth of a shallow ravine where a seepage of water offered a little moisture and the steep sides some shelter from the blazing sun.

VIII

Their new camp was surrounded by a rough, jutting plateau from which the larger hills climbed in terraced steps toward the massive crests beyond. To their right, some ten or fifteen miles away, a mountain with a pronounced saddle pushed its double head up out of the jumbled débris of some forgotten volcanic action.

Bill Drake studied it, then pulled the map from his sweat-damp shirt. He spread it on the ground, leaning forward over it. Finally he refolded the paper and thrust it back into his shirt.

Mary Thorne had been standing not far away, watching the play of changing expression on his face, and she stepped in now, saying in an eager voice: "Are we on the right trail?"

Drake shrugged expressively. "Who knows? This country changes with every cloudburst. Half the time a man can't backtrack himself. I once knew a miner who left his claim and went fifteen miles for supplies. When he returned, he found his cañon buried under a hundred feet of loose rock and mud. If that has happened to your wagon train, we'll never find it."

He turned away and the girl stared after him, irritated and dissatisfied. For an instant she was tempted to follow him, then, changing her mind, she turned back to the wagon and let the cook fill her plate. This she carried to a small sandy patch at the right of the camp where a cluster of waist-high rocks offered a little privacy. Here she settled herself, her position partially obscured by the bordering rocks from the camp below, and proceeded to eat unhurriedly.

After she finished, she set the plate aside and leaned back, pulling her hat down to shade her eyes. She was not asleep, but her tired body seemed to vibrate with waves of weariness, making her a little light-headed. She lay there, almost too exhausted to move, until finally she sensed that she was no longer alone. Opening her eyes slowly, she stared up to find the Pecos Kid squatted on the rocks, not six feet away, watching her.

His pale eyes were steady and unblinking. The eyelashes were so light as to be almost invisible. This gave a certain reptilian quality to his stare, and the girl shivered unconsciously.

She closed her eyes, hoping that he would go away, but the feeling of his presence lingered, and she reopened them. The Pecos Kid had not altered his position. His long, narrow face wore an intent look, as if he were staring at something in the far distance. There was a hypnotic quality about his stare, and Mary Thorne had to rouse herself consciously to break it. She straightened.

"You want something?"

"You," said the Kid, and his thin lips parted in the coldest smile she had ever seen.

She caught her breath, nagging fear struggling with rising anger. But the anger won. "Get away from here. You're crazy."

I've been talking to Gordon," he said. "Gordon told me you want to make a deal. Gordon says you're afraid of Drake."

The words caught her off balance. She was torn by her desire to make friends with the crew and her deep-felt aversion for this grinning man who looked like a death's head, squatting there, leering at her.

She forced down her feeling of repugnance and managed to say in a more even tone: "Whatever

Mister Gordon told you is probably correct, but it isn't safe for you to be seen talking to me."

"Why?"

She was exasperated. "That should be pretty obvious to anyone who isn't a fool. If Bill Drake sees you, we'll both be in trouble."

"To hell with Bill Drake." For a year and a half since joining the crew, the Pecos Kid had resented Bill Drake. The Kid, like most of his kind, was an egomaniac. He was certain that he was the most deadly man on the frontier, that his hand could pull one of the heavy guns faster than anyone in the territory. He resented orders of any kind, and many a night, lying stretched out on the hard ground, he had planned for the day when he and Drake would have their showdown.

But with all this, there was a streak of hard caution in the Kid, a caution born of his early childhood. This caution had enabled him to survive as long as he had, and it was this caution that had held him a restive, but apparently amenable follower of Drake's leadership. He had bided his time, studying the men around Drake, awaiting his chance to strike at the leader. Long before this he had measured Monte Gordon, spotting the man's weaknesses, planning that, when the time came, he could use Gordon, even as Gordon was now hoping to use him.

He had not been deceived by Gordon's words of the preceding night. He knew exactly what

Gordon hoped. Gordon hoped to pit him against Drake, and, after he had killed the outlaw chief, Gordon expected to step forward and take control.

The Kid had no aversion to killing Drake. The man who killed Bill Drake probably would be the most famous gunfighter on the frontier, but once the killing was an accomplished fact, he did not mean to step aside for Gordon. He would take over the leadership of the crew himself.

This, then, had been a dream of long standing, and unconsciously Mary Thorne, by her presence, had brought it to a head. Also, she had done something to the Pecos Kid. He had hated and mistrusted women for a long time, and he mistrusted this girl. But in the quiet minutes while he watched her, thinking that she slept, something had stirred in his narrow breast. Suddenly he wanted her. He wanted her as he had never wanted any of the dance-hall girls, any of the whores who had served in his passing fancies. There was something cruel in his wanting, something perverted. He wanted to hurt her, to strip her naked, and beat her with a whip, and watch her writhe as he spent his hatred and venom for all women on her well-shaped body. But he wanted to take her, also. He wanted to master her, to ravish her, and then have her come crawling to him, begging for mercy that he would never give. This built up in him, turning his thoughts hot and surging until there seemed to be a red film over them, dimming his vision. He was suddenly without fear of any kind, without the ability to judge, to wait for more proper surroundings. He wanted the girl and he wanted her now, and, if it meant a showdown with Bill Drake, he was ready.

He rose, all in one motion, and he moved in toward her. He grinned, meaning to be reassuring, but it had the opposite effect on Mary Thorne. She tried to come to her feet, but one of the Kid's long arms snaked out and his fingers wrapped themselves about her waist. She tried to draw her gun with her free hand, but she had waited too long. The Kid laughed down at her, knocking it aside easily, with a contempt that told that he considered it not much more than a toy. She hit him in the face then, not with her open hand, but her fist, striking like a boy, her small knuckles hard and sharp, bruising his curved lips.

He swore at her, dragging her toward him, crushing her against him, careless of any hurt he might give, swearing savagely under his breath. "You're like all women," he said. "You can't be trusted. You can't keep a bargain." He buried his mouth against hers as she opened her lips to scream.

Andy Drake came down off the rock pile. In one swinging leap he landed just behind the Kid, his left hand shooting out to grasp the Kid's bony shoulder. He jerked the Pecos Kid away from the girl so violently that she was pulled forward to her knees. Then he swung his fist directly into the Kid's narrow face.

The Kid stumbled backwards, trying to regain his balance. His high heel caught on a rock fragment and threw him heavily. He fell on his back, the wind partly knocked out of him, glaring up at Andy, trying to claw with both hands at his holstered guns.

Andy dived, landing on top of the thin chest, driving the air from the slight body with his very bulk. He reached down, caught the man's right wrist, and dragged the clawing fingers clear to the gun. He twisted the arm upward and outward until the elbow threatened to spring from the socket.

The Kid groaned, but he was no man to quit. He still struggled to free himself, to wrench clear of Andy's superior strength.

Andy panted: "Stop it or I'll break your arm."

"Break it, damn you!" The Pecos Kid heaved desperately.

Andy gave the arm a final twist. Beads of sweat jumped out on the Kid's forehead. His eyes closed. His face went dead white under the heavy tan, and then all the strength seemed to flow out of him.

In that instant Andy released the arm, reached down, and pulled the Kid's guns. He rose, pointing one of the guns at its owner. Somehow the Kid found the strength to drag himself upright, also. He charged, spitting like a cat.

Andy did not shoot. Instead he side-stepped the blind charge, swung the heavy gun, and brought its long barrel down across the thin man's head.

The Pecos Kid's arms went wide. He dropped to his knees. Andy beat him to the ground, striking savagely until the Kid lay stretched out, face down. Not until the twitching body had ceased to move did Andy step back. He used his sleeve to wipe the sweat from his forehead. Breathing heavily, he stared down at the unconscious gunman.

Below them the camp was in turmoil. Men charged up the slight slope. Still holding the guns, he turned to look at them. Then he glanced at the girl. It had all happened so rapidly that she was still on her knees. She scrambled up hastily as he said: "Hurt, Bantam?"

She shook her head and his mouth twisted. "What did you have to make up to that dog for?" He used the toe of his boot to stir the senseless Kid.

A denial leaped to her lips, and two angry spots of color burned in her cheeks. But she crowded down the words of denial. "You're the one who said I should pick a strong man to protect me," she panted.

Andy's lips curled at the corners. "I don't admire your taste, Bantam."

She winced, then threw the words at him: "Is there a choice between murderers?"

142

He looked at her for a moment longer, but, before he had a chance to speak, the crew, led by Bill Drake, boiled through the rocks and surrounded them.

Drake checked their rush and advanced alone. He stared at the unconscious Kid, at his silent brother, and at the girl. Finally he turned and surveyed the assembled crew. "Any of you care to pick up this fight?" he said tonelessly. He faced them all, but his main attention was centered on Monte Gordon.

Gordon knew it. Gordon shifted uncertainly from one foot to the other, not meeting Drake's stare, trying to make up his mind. Silently he was cursing the Pecos Kid for having made his move so soon and so ill-timed. They weren't ready. They weren't organized. They stood no chance of removing Drake at the moment.

Drake watched him coolly, as if he could read what was passing through Gordon's mind. His mouth twisted in a little sardonic smile. Still holding his eyes on Gordon's face, he addressed the other men. "Catch up this piece of carrion and cart him back to the fire."

Tex Hart and Burns stepped up, grasping the Kid under the arms and by the legs. Between them, they carried his slack body down the slope. The rest of the crew hesitated for a moment, then followed. Gordon was the last to retreat.

Bill did not move. He stood perfectly still until

they had reached the cañon floor. Then he turned to face his brother. "You should have killed him when you had the chance," Bill Drake said. "You're green yet. An experienced man would never use his hands on a killer like the Kid. Men like Pecos don't understand that kind of fighting. He'll put a bullet in your back the first chance he gets. Haven't you got any sense?"

Andy stood sullenly under the lash. "He was mauling Bantam."

"Who?"

Andy reddened. "That's what I call her," he said.

Bill Drake looked at Mary Thorne. "I wish that none of us had ever seen you, ma'am," he said in a slow, deliberate voice.

Mary Thorne returned his stare defiantly although the color in her cheeks deepened. In the last moments her fear of this big man had become secondary to her fear of the Pecos Kid and others. In his own way, Bill Drake stood for authority, authority against unbridled lawlessness.

"What makes you say that?" she asked at last.

"You know why. You're raising hell with my crew. I've watched you when you didn't know I was watching. The Kid is a dog, but he would never have moved against you today unless he believed you didn't dare refuse him. You're a fool. These men aren't tame puppies to be stopped by a woman's haughty glance. Some of them haven't been in a town for six months. Some of them have almost forgotten what a woman looks like. And now you come along and deliberately stir them up."

Her face flamed. "You have no right to talk like that!"

"Haven't I?" he said. "If I haven't the right, I'm making it my right. This is my crew. We're in the middle of hostile Indian country. We haven't a friend within fifty miles. If we get to fighting among ourselves, we're dead. If I see you so much as smile at one of the crew again, I'll tie you up in the chuck wagon. Now get some sleep. We're riding out before dark." He wheeled on his brother. "Come with me. I want to talk to you."

Andy glanced at the girl, but she refused to meet his eyes. He followed Bill down the slope.

Bill halted before he reached the fire. "I don't know what I'm going to do with you," he said. "Look over there." He pointed toward a high range of distant hills. "See that?"

Andy looked. Three columns of smoke were rising straight into the quiet, hot air. "Indians?"

Bill nodded. "If you had been paying more attention to what you are supposed to be doing and less to that crazy girl, you'd have seen them before this. They've been watching us since yesterday. There's damn' little goes on in these hills that they don't know about."

"White River?"

Bill shrugged. "Maybe. Maybe some of Victorio's

men. Maybe only some broncos out stealing horses. It doesn't matter. As long as we keep together, we're all right. But if we should split up, we'll all lose our hair. Those Indians have some old scores to settle with my men. For a dollar I'd turn around and head south, but the crowd wouldn't go. They're dreaming of that gold."

Andy started to answer, but Bill did not give him the chance. He spun on his heel, moving into the camp. After a minute's hesitation while he stared at the distant columns of smoke, Andy followed.

IX

It was dusk when they rode northward. Bill Drake was purposely crossing the broken country at night, saving the strength of both animals and men.

Eastward the Dragoons faded as they bore away to miss Fort Grant and come to the Gila west of its junction with the San Pedro. To the north, the mountains turned cindery, losing their thin vegetation in a welter of wasted, heat-scorched rocks. Near midnight they struck water, and Bill Drake gave the reluctant order to step down.

At first he had been in no hurry to proceed, but now he was consumed with a desire to forge ahead as rapidly as possible. The crew seemed to share his feeling of hurry, or restlessness and worry.

They were glum, silent, watchful as they chewed the jerked meat and the cold beans that the cook dished out.

Afterward, all save the horse guards stretched flat against the rocky ground, ignoring the gathering chill as if too beat out to think or care. No one, save the old cook, had wasted a word on Mary Thorne since the ride had begun. She felt the weight of their questioning glances, of the sullenness as if they collectively blamed her for their being in this place.

She stayed close to the wagon, for she, too, had seen those smoke signals drawing warning in the fading afternoon sky. Not until the darkness covered the rising pillars were they lost to sight. But instead of bringing relief, the covering darkness only added to her feeling of danger.

Across the fire Andy Drake also sat by himself. He, too, felt the crew's dislike. He knew that to them, he was an outsider and that, although few of them actually liked the Pecos Kid, they would take the Kid's side if the quarrel continued.

Bill Drake knew this, also. He leaned against the tailgate of the wagon, talking to the cook, but watching every movement in the camp. Suddenly he raised his voice. "Kid!"

The Pecos Kid had been sitting beside the fire between Monte Gordon and Tex Hart. His head was bandaged, he cradled his useless arm, but he could not have failed to hear Bill's call. Yet he gave no sign. His elbows were on his knees and he was staring at the ground between his booted feet.

The lagging conversation around the fire died entirely. The crew watched Bill without appearing to. Bill Drake stood for a moment as if he had been turned to stone. Then he moved forward slowly. He did not stop until he stood directly over the Pecos Kid. "Get up," he said.

The Kid did not stir. He might have been deaf, for all the sign he gave.

Bill Drake looked around. He caught Monte's eyes upon him, malice-filled and mocking; he saw Tex Hart shift slightly in order to free the gun at his hip. And he ignored them. He reached down, caught the Pecos Kid by the collar of his coat, and hoisted him to his feet. "When I speak to you," he said, "stand up."

With an oath, the Pecos Kid tried to pull himself free. At the same time he reached for one of his guns.

Bill Drake did not release him. Instead, he lifted the Kid off the ground and shook him as a terrier might shake a mouse.

The Kid managed to get one gun free, but Drake had him twisted around so that it was impossible for the Kid to put a bullet into the older man.

Drake held him easily, big muscles bulging in his right arm as he extended it, still supporting the struggling Kid. "Behave," he said, "or I'll break your neck." His hand shot out, wrenched the gun from the Kid's grasp, and dropped it in the dust. He reached around the slim waist, hugging the Kid back against him, and got the second gun. Then he dropped the Kid.

Pecos landed on his feet like a balanced cat. He turned, spitting like a cat as rage filled him. His thin face was marked by his fight with Andy that afternoon. The rough bandage had come loose, slipping down over one ear, and his light eyes fairly smoked. "Let me have a gun," he said in a phlegm-ropy snarl.

Bill Drake looked at him and there was contempt in his eyes. "I'd like to kill you," he said slowly, distinctly, so that no one man around the fire could fail to hear. "I'd be doing the whole territory a favor if I put a bullet in your wishbone."

"Go ahead." The Kid stared down at his guns, lying in the flinty dust at has feet. "Go ahead, kill me." He dropped, even as he spoke, falling purposely on his injured left arm, his right hand snaking out for the nearest gun. He touched it, but he never got it fully into his grasp.

Bill Drake, making no attempt to draw his own weapon, stepped in, bringing his heel down on the back of the Kid's hand. He twisted, his whole weight fully on the turning heel. The Kid cried out in anguish as the bones fractured under the grinding heel. Bill Drake gave it an added twist, and stepped back. The Kid writhed on the ground like a wounded snake.

Drake watched him for a moment in utter silence. Then he said: "Get up." The Kid did not obey, and Bill caught him again by the collar. "Get up when I tell you to or I'll break your other hand." He jerked the Kid erect, leaving him to stand swaying, staring stupidly at his shattered hand.

"Maybe you won't be so quick to pull your gun now," Drake said. After that he looked directly at Monte Gordon. There was no mockery in Gordon's eyes now, only a deep-seated, cringing fear.

He met Drake's stare for the moment, then let his gaze fall away. Drake shrugged. "Take care of him," he said, and walked over to his brother's side.

The Kid tried to shake free. His eyes met Gordon's, wanting the other man to take up the fight. But Gordon just motioned to Tex Hart for help. Tex came to Gordon's assistance, and together they forced the shaken man toward the spring.

Surprisingly Mary Thorne had come to her feet. She walked over to Drake and said in a tone that was loud enough for all to hear: "You brute. You're nothing but a brute." She turned then and followed Gordon and Hart, coming up to them as they lowered the Kid to a sitting position beside the spring.

"Here, let me help." She bent beside the injured

man, taking the bruised hand in both her own, washing it gently, then feeling the jagged bones. "We'll have to try and set it. Has someone got some cloth?"

The cook had, in his wagon. He brought it, and one of the men was trying to whittle out some splints.

Andy watched the operations without moving, saying to his brother in an undertone: "You've made no extra friends tonight."

"No," said Bill. "We've both made a mistake . . . you for not killing him this afternoon, and me for not breaking both his hands tonight. He'll come at one or both of us yet."

"And he'll have men behind him."

Bill nodded. "That's a woman for you. You jumped in to protect her this afternoon, and this evening she's busy playing nurse merely because that dog is hurt. She forgets whose fault it was that he got hurt, and, if she thinks the Kid is changed because of a few broken bones, she knows nothing about him. He's as trustworthy as a rattlesnake and just as poisonous. To hell with her, and him." He started back toward the fire. "All right, throw the Kid in the wagon. It's time to roll."

Mary Thorne had just finished tying the improvised splints in place. The Kid had not uttered a sound all the time her strong fingers had worked at the fractured hand, but his face looked very white and there was a line of perspiration across his narrow forehead.

She stood up, knocked the dust from her knees, and marched over to face Bill. "That man is in no condition to move."

Bill stared at her. "What do you want me to do, leave him here? He'll be lucky if the cook will let him ride in the wagon. It's up to the cook. If he doesn't, the Kid can ride or rot here for all of me." He turned away without interest.

Mary Thorne looked after him, unbelieving, then slowly went over to where the cook was loading his gear. "You heard what Bill said?"

The cook was torn between his growing respect for the girl and his dislike of having his wagon arrangements disturbed. He had no liking for the Pecos Kid and he pretended none. "I'll let him ride if you say so," he grumbled. "But tell him to keep his feet out of the food box or I'll break both his legs."

Tex Hart and Monte Gordon helped the Pecos Kid into the chuck wagon, made him as com- fortable as possible, and mounted their own horses. The crew moved out, the girl riding beside the swaying wagon, Monte Gordon and Hart directly behind her.

Gordon spoke to his friend in an undertone so low that it barely carried above the scuff of the horses' hoofs. "Did you see how the girl came to help the Kid when he was hurt? She's smart."

Hart turned in his saddle. "What are you driving at?"

"The way she stood up to Drake. She called him a brute. The whole business was the best thing that could have happened for us. Every man in the crew is blaming Drake for the fight. When the final showdown comes, they'll all line up with us."

At the head of the column Andy was saying almost the same thing. "I don't like the way the crew acted while you were roughing the Kid. They're about ready to cross you, Bill."

"That's right," said his brother. His eyes were on the distant mountains. "There hasn't been a day since we started riding that one of them wouldn't have jumped me if they dared."

"And it's probably my fault." Andy sounded defensive. "I put her up to it, I guess."

"What are you talking about?"

Andy stopped. He still did not want to tell his brother that the girl had seen Wakeman's horse with blood on the saddle.

Bill waited, then said with a short laugh: "No one put her up to making a play for Gordon or the Pecos Kid unless you think she did it to make you jealous. Look," Bill said, "don't ask me why a woman wants to do anything. I've stopped guessing about them a long time ago. And stop worrying about things you can't help. The chances are that none of us will get out of these hills with our hair. If that's true, there's nothing much to worry about that counts."

"You don't believe that."

"Son," said Bill, "I learned about life a long time ago. A lot of people think I've got sand. They're wrong. I decided sometime back that one of these days I was going to die. Maybe it will be tonight. Maybe it will be tomorrow. What the hell difference does it make, so why worry about it."

"I'm not ready to die yet," Andy told him. "I've got a lot to live for."

"What?" said Bill. "A lot of hard riding and thirst and sweat and fleas. Oh, I know, when I was your age, hell itself couldn't hold me. The world was open and wide and I started out to get mine. It wasn't as much fun as I thought. I guess maybe it never was as much fun."

Andy had never seen his brother in this mood before. "But there are a lot of things ahead of you," he argued. "What about the gold? If we find it, you and I could go someplace with our share. We could buy a ranch and settle down. We could do a lot of things."

"Sure," said Bill, "a hundred things." He spurred ahead as if he no longer wanted to talk about it.

Andy did not follow. Instead he dropped back, reining his horse in at the girl's side.

She gave no sign that she was conscious of his presence, and they rode thus for a couple of miles.

Gordon and Tex Hart had fallen back when Andy arrived so that they could talk without Andy's hearing what they said.

Andy waited for her to break the silence. When she did not, he said: "I suppose you're very proud of yourself."

"I have no interest in your opinion of me or my actions," Mary Thorne told him.

"Haven't you?" Andy said. "That was a nice little piece of acting on your part, tying up the Kid's broken hand."

"That wasn't acting." Her tone was sharp. "Anyone would want to help a man who is hurt."

"And why did the Kid get hurt?" Andy sounded bitter. "Why did I have to jump him this afternoon? You know why. I couldn't stand by and watch him paw you. My God, Bantam, get some sense. The Pecos Kid is a loco fool. If you once let him lay hands on you, there'll be no stopping him. What are you trying to do, get raped?"

"I can take care of myself," she flashed at him. "Besides, that doesn't excuse your brother for what he did tonight."

"And you're loco, too," Andy said. "You don't even understand what Bill did. I should have killed the Kid this afternoon. I didn't, and the Kid will never forgive the fact that I manhandled him, especially before you. His pride is all he's got, and I tore his pride to bits. The chances are that he would have shot me in the back the first time he had the chance. Bill stopped that. Bill figures I'm not fast enough with a gun to beat the Kid. That's why he deliberately picked the fight tonight. He was trying to transfer the Kid's hatred to himself." She did not answer as he raced on. "And this is all a part of a nice neat little plan you have. I saw you talking to Gordon this afternoon, and then I saw Gordon talking to the Kid. Crazy as he is, the Kid would never have jumped you this after- noon, unless something had stirred him up. Bill knows that, and I know it. We both realize you're deliberately throwing yourself at the men, trying to break up the crew. That's pretty cheap, Bantam. It's what I'd expect of a saloon woman or a cheap dance-hall girl."

She was so angry that she found it difficult to speak. She said in a choked voice: "I'm only doing what you suggested, you fool. You told me to pick a man to protect me. I picked Gordon. Would you rather I'd made another choice?"

He did not answer, riding ahead in silence, realizing that he was caught between his rising feelings for this girl and his new-found loyalty to his brother. He was not certain what his feelings toward Mary Thorne were. At times he hated her, and this was one of those moments.

Damn her, he thought. *She twists every word that I say to her. She always manages to put me in the wrong.* To avoid looking at her, he concentrated on where they were going and realized those up ahead were moving into a small draw.

The banks of the draw shelved away on either side to be lost in the purple, velvety darkness that now softened the harsh land, masking the jutting rock dykes, hiding the jumbled masses of boulders.

They were still too low for timber, but the slopes were well blanketed with mescal bushes and clumps of mesquite. Cat-claw bushes with their sharp, fish-hook barbs pressed close on either side so that they snagged at the passing riders and the sides of the lumbering wagon.

The night was quiet and peaceful and serene, nothing to alert the senses nor warn the riders, nothing until an arrow came out of the brush and cut Burns clear out of his saddle. He dropped to the ground, then struggled to his feet, a cry of horror welling up out of his throat as he tugged at the feather-head end that showed in his shirt front like a decoration.

A gun exploded, then another. A horse went down. Monte Gordon, who had been riding beside Burns, rose in his stirrups, firing toward the flashes of guns in the brush beside the trail and at the same time sending out his warning shout to the crew.

"*Apaches! Apaches!*"

X

The crew reacted at once, like the trained fighters they were. There was none of the panic that the Indians had apparently hoped for. They wheeled for cover and Bill Drake's voice cut along the line. "Watch the horses! Watch the horses!" Bill Drake knew his Indians. He had been fighting them for years and he felt that this was no war party in strength. An Indian seldom fights at night, fearing that, if he dies, his spirit will fail to find its way to the hunting ground.

This was more likely a mere horse-stealing sortie, a few broncos out to cause enough confusion so that they could steal the spare horses of the crew.

He drove directly into the brush in an attempt to flank the attackers, followed closely by Andy and Monte Gordon. The rest of the crew was attempting to protect the chuck wagon and the horse herd.

Apparently the Indians had few guns, for only scattering shots dropped among the defenders. As he crashed through the shoulder-high brush, Andy caught movement, not much clearer than a shadow, and saw a brave rise directly in the path of his horse. He fired at the Apache's face and watched the man go down as he drove past.

The night behind him was full of sound—men's cries, the sharp, piercing whinny of a horse in pain. Off to his right, he heard his brother swear. He spurred toward Bill, only to be ordered back.

The attack had failed. There were no more shots from the brush and Bill ordered him to rejoin the train, reining in his own horse as he shouted across the night. Bill knew the dangers of riding through the brush.

Andy retraced his route, expecting to find the body of the dead Indian. But there was no sign of it. Apparently the man had not been so seriously injured that he could not drag himself away.

At the first sign of the attack, the cook had shouted to Mary Thorne, ordering her to get down under the wagon. Then he had hauled his heavy rifle from its place beside the seat and watched the bordering brush, searching out something at which to shoot. But nothing had moved in the deceptive shadows. Apparently the attack had shifted toward the horse herd, for the cook heard sharp firing from the rear.

The girl had disobeyed him. She had swung out of her saddle, but, instead of seeking shelter under the wagon, she had walked boldly to where Burns lay, unmoving, beside the trail. Reaching him, she knelt quickly, only to learn that he was dead.

The cook left the wagon to join her and grunted softly when he looked down at Burns. He had seen death in many forms, and he was so close to it that it no longer held much terror for him.

"Get back to the wagon," he had told her. "I think they've faded, but you can't be sure. You make a pretty target, standing there."

She had gone without protest, feeling a little sick. Death still had its terror for her and she was not able to shake off a lingering despondency that made her feel that they were all doomed.

"You can't be sure they're gone," she murmured.

The cook leaned his rifle against the tailgate of the wagon. "No, but an Injun don't care much for battle at night, and, if they were going to take us, they'd have charged in before now. I'd guess that it was a small band, hungry for horses."

Andy, followed by Bill Drake and Gordon, rode up to the wagon. A moment later the rest of the crew came drifting back, leading the spare horses.

"How many hurt?"

"Burns is dead." The cook's tone expressed no grief.

Tex Hart spoke from beyond the wagon. "Youngman got an arrow in his shoulder . . . Field caught a bullet in the leg. Neither is bad hurt."

Bill looked at the girl. There was the edge of mockery in his tone. "Chance for you to try some of your nursing," he said, and turned to Andy. "You and Gordon circle and see what sign you can pick up. We'll stay here until daylight. Don't get separated, and don't get more than fifty yards from the trail."

They moved their horses against the rising grade, and reëntered the brush, keeping a good ten yards apart. They rode upward toward the lips of the draw until they came against the naked rock of the rim. Careful not to rise high enough so that they would be outlined against the lighter sky, they edged forward, handguns ready, watchful yet already certain that the Indians had gone, slipping through the barrier of broken stones toward the higher ridges above.

They came to a place where the savages' horses had been held, and Gordon swung down to look at the tracks. He said there could not have been more than five or six. He found blood on one of the stones, and Andy guessed that this was from the one he had nicked.

Gordon was just remounting when the sudden scream slapped at them out of the night—a woman's scream, wordless, yet carrying a quality of fear that lifted the short hairs at the back of Andy's neck. The scream was followed almost at once by the pounding explosion of a heavy rifle. By the time the shot came, Andy had already swung his horse and was driving down through the prickly brush toward the camp below.

Behind him, he heard a crash as Gordon followed. He heard the other man swearing, and then he broke out into the clearness of the trail and had a moment's panoramic view of the whole crew, motionless, held thus by surprise.

The scene was lighted by a couple of lanterns that the cook had hung on the wagon so he could tend to the wounded. Mary Thorne was standing to one side, frozen and motionless. The cook, half turned as if he had been headed for the horse herd when the action took place, was also motionless.

Bill Drake, flat on the ground, did not move while the Pecos Kid stood over him, gripping the cook's rifle with his undamaged hand.

Andy jabbed his spurs into his horse without stopping to think. The animal leaped toward the wagon, the crew members jumping for safety as he charged straight at the Kid.

The Kid heard him coming and swung around. He had the rifle cradled across his useless arm. He fired without bringing it fully up, the stock held against his thigh. The .50-caliber slug stuck Andy's horse directly in the mouth, tearing upward into the animal's brain. The horse fell as if it had been hit in the head by an axe, and Andy went down with it. He had been carrying his six-gun in his hand, and, as he landed on his shoulder, the gun leaped from his grasp, vanishing somewhere in the dust. As he fell, he rolled over on one shoulder, then onto his hands and knees. He came upright with a lunge, a dozen feet separating him from the crouching Kid. He jumped forward. The heavy gun roared again and the bullet tore the hat from Andy's head, sending it spinning in the dust, but leaving him untouched.

The recoil kicked the rifle almost out of the Pecos Kid's grasp, and saved Andy's life. Before the Kid would get the rifle leveled again, Andy was on top of him, tearing the gun from his hand and hurling it into the brush beside the trail.

But the Pecos Kid was far from through. He had stolen a butcher knife from the cook's box and he wore it now, thrust into his belt. He pulled it with his good hand and came in at a half crouch, his maimed arm held straight out before him. Andy might have dodged, but was blind with anger. He charged straight in, brushing aside the broken hand and making a grab for the knife wrist. The Kid dropped sidewise, kicking out one leg, hooking it between Andy's knees and tripping him.

Despite the disadvantage of the broken hand the Kid was confident. He was a trained barroom fighter. He knew every trick and he had the knife while Andy had only his bare hands. He grinned wolfishly as they fell together. Then his lips opened and his teeth closed firmly on Andy's ear. He had Andy's right arm pinned between them, and he swung at Andy's left side with the knife. The sharp blade tore through the shirt and cut a shallow groove between Andy's ribs.

But Andy's strength was greater than the Kid had realized. He managed to tear loose, disregarding the pain from his damaged ear. He got his right elbow into the Kid's stomach. Using what leverage he could, he forced their bodies apart to free his arm. He took another knife cut in the shoulder as he did so, but managed to get a real grip on the knife wrist. He twisted the Kid's arm out and up, and then backwards, trying to force the man to drop the knife. But the Pecos Kid clung to it grimly, beating Andy about the head with his splinted hand.

The crew had formed a rough semicircle, but no one, save the cook, made any attempt to interfere. Pop had stepped forward, but Monte Gordon dragged him back.

"Let them fight," Monte growled.

The cook stared at him hotly, but Pop was an old man and he knew it. He lowered his eyes, hating Gordon and hating himself.

Andy was conscious of nothing save the Pecos Kid. He was grasping the wrist, twisting, trying to shake the knife loose, and all the time taking a beating about the head. The sharp edge of the wooden splint had cut his forehead and the blood ran down into his eye as he increased his pressure on the knife arm. He tried desperately to force the Pecos Kid to release his grip, but still he could not get enough leverage. He arched his body, managing to sit up, bringing the knife arm around in front of him. But the Kid twisted like a snake, rolling over, managing somehow to break Andy's grip as he came up to his knees. Andy swung around to face him, and for an instant they rested thus, glaring at each other before the Kid threw himself forward, thrusting the knife as if it had been a short sword.

Andy fell sidewise, avoiding the thrust. The Kid, overbalanced, fell heavily on his face. But he rolled quickly to his back, pointing the knife upright to keep Andy away while he struggled to rise. But this time Andy was ready. He shot to his feet, caught the injured arm, and threw the Kid cleanly over his head. The Kid fell, his knife under him. He lay there motionlessly.

Andy dashed the blood out of his eyes and looked around. The old cook stepped in and shoved a gun at him. He took it, staring down at it stupidly for an instant as if he had never seen a gun before. Then he stepped forward, straightening his shoulders. He stirred the Kid's limp body with his boot toe.

"Get up," he said.

The Pecos Kid failed to move. Andy was about to kick him in the ribs when something in the way the Kid's body was twisted caught his attention. He hesitated for an instant, then took half a step backward.

"Turn him over," he told the cook.

It was Tex Hart who obeyed, and, as he lifted the body, they all saw the knife handle sticking out from the left breast, its broad blade entirely buried in the Kid's chest.

Someone across the circle swore, but Andy never took his attention from the Kid's face. "Is he dead?"

Hart had knelt to make a quick examination. He looked up, nodding, and there was anger in his big face.

But Andy ignored Hart. He lifted his eyes and stared directly at Monte Gordon, seeing the hunger in the man's eyes, the wild eagerness. "You want a part of this, Monte?" He faced the man squarely as he lowered the cook's gun into the empty holster at his side.

It was not fear that held Monte Gordon motionlessly. The eagerness was still in his eyes and each watching man knew that he would have liked nothing better than to have pulled his gun. But something held him back. This, he sensed, was not the time for him to move if he wished to carry the crew along with him, and he made his voice sound almost pleasant when he said: "Not my fight."

"All right," Andy said. "Don't forget it." He did not take his attention from Gordon's face, but he spoke to the cook. "What about Bill?"

The cook had been bending over Bill. He straightened and his face looked almost as if he had been crying. "It was my fault. I shouldn't have left that rifle where the Kid could reach it. I shouldn't . . . I shouldn't . . ."

He was interrupted by a voice from the trampled

ground at his feet. "Stop that caterwauling and give me a hand."

The crew stared at the fallen leader. Bill Drake was not dead. He was twisting his heavy body, trying to get his knees under him, but he failed until Andy and the cook jumped forward to give him a hand. Then he stood shakily on his feet, grasping at the wagon for support with his right hand. His left shoulder was bathed in blood that had run down to stain the full side of his shirt.

Andy held him steady while the cook dragged out a box for him to sit on. Together they eased him down gently as the rest of the crew crowded around. Mary Thorne pushed her way through the circle. Her face was very white and her eyes looked enormous, but her voice was steady as she said: "Let me."

No one stopped her. With Andy's help she cut away the bloody shirt and exposed the wound. The heavy slug had smashed through the shoulder, leaving a bruised and gaping hole where it had entered and a larger one where it had torn out the heavy back muscles.

Bill was wan, weak, and dizzy from loss of blood. To Andy he looked as if he were already dying.

"We'd better turn back and try to get him to the doctor at Fort Grant," Andy said in an undertone.

"No, you don't." Bill's voice was weak, but it still carried its old authority. "Get me to the fort and they'll find a good reason for putting a rope collar around my neck. Patch it up the best you can . . . and throw me in the wagon. I've been hit worse before now and pulled through."

Mary Thorne had been carefully examining the wound. "You're a fool," she told him tensely. "What do you want to do, die?"

The mocking light showed for an instant in Bill's eyes. "Isn't that what you've been working for?"

"And do you blame me?" She met his eyes squarely, then ignored him. She said to the cook: "Can you find a clean shirt somewhere?"

The cook produced one that he had been saving carefully at the bottom of his box. It was, he explained a little sheepishly, his burying shirt. He had kept it so that he could be dressed properly for his own funeral.

Mary Thorne tore the shirt into rough strips and fashioned a crude bandage, but, although she worked with a quick sure touch, it was full daylight before they lifted the wounded man and placed him on the rude bunk in the wagon.

Next she turned to the other wounded, finding that none of their hurts was as serious. Burns and the Pecos Kid were buried under a small cairn of stones, and finally the silent crew swung wearily back into their saddles, each deep in his own thoughts, his own fears. They were long accustomed to following Bill's leadership. Now that he rode wounded in the wagon, they had a sense of loss. Many of them had cursed him bitterly in the past, and some would have turned on him had they dared, but now each one wondered what would happen if he failed to recover.

Even Mary Thorne was filled with alarming doubts. Much as she feared and hated him, there had been something comforting in merely seeing Bill's big figure riding stoically and unafraid at the head of the column. She tried to voice her feeling to Andy as they took the trail, but she found that it was curiously hard for her to talk to the younger Drake. At first it had seemed so easy, for she had recognized something of her own quick spirit in this man. Beside the other outlaws, he appeared friendly and concerned with her welfare. But all that had changed within the last twenty-four hours. He was withdrawn, unhelpful, grim, and silent.

"I'm sorry about your brother," she said, and tried to make her tone sound meek. The last thing she wanted at the moment was to quarrel with Andy. She knew that, in part, he blamed her for what had happened, and at the moment she was willing to take some of the blame if only to receive a kind word in return.

Andy turned his head to look at her. They were riding beside the wagon while Monte Gordon and Tex Hart rode at the head of the column.

Monte Gordon did not regret that Bill Drake was hurt. In fact his only regret was that Bill still lived. But he meant to assert his leadership now, and he had done so by the mere act of taking the position at the head of the column.

Mary Thorne had expected that Andy would object, that Andy would try and claim his brother's place. But so far he had given no sign that he was even conscious of what Gordon was doing. He looked at the girl carefully now and his expression showed that he did not believe her.

"Are you?" he said coldly.

She flushed, striving to crowd down quickly rising anger, knowing that despite her efforts she and Andy were quarreling again. Why was it that they seemed unable to speak to each other without argument?

"I *am* sorry about your brother," she told him, biting off the words. "I am perfectly selfish about it. I was afraid of him, but I'm more afraid of what this country will do to us without him to lead the crew. I'm afraid of the Indians. I'm afraid we won't find the gold, and I'm afraid that we'll die of thirst. I don't trust Monte Gordon to lead us. I think he's a fool."

"You should have thought of all this before you made up to Gordon," Andy said.

"It was you who told me what to do."

"Oh, so now it's my fault."

"Look." She was still trying desperately to ride

170

down her temper. "We're acting like a couple of kids. This is not the time for us to quarrel. Can't we both admit that we were wrong and forget it?"

Andy's eyes did not soften as he looked at her. "Bill warned me never to try to guess what a woman is up to. But I'd like to know. What have you got in mind now, Bantam? You've got what you thought you wanted yesterday. Gordon is riding at the head of the crew. That's the way you planned it, but now you seem to have changed your mind. What's the matter, did you make a deal with Gordon that you're afraid you'll have to keep?"

Had she been close enough she would have struck him across the face. He had so exactly guessed her fears. "All right." Her voice was cold now, almost deadly. "You're right. I did make a deal with Monte Gordon. You suggested it when you told me to pick one of the men and cling to him." She paused, forcing herself to admit the truth. "I shouldn't have done it." She paused. It was hard to admit the fault. Then more softly, but firmly she continued: "But I want to tell you one thing, Mister Andrew Drake. I'm not the kind of person who clings to anyone. I stand on my own feet and I fight. Unfortunately I haven't the weight and the bulging muscles to stand up and swing with a man. I have to use my head, and I used it the best I could. I figured that no one man was big enough to stand up and protect me against the crew, so I started out to make every one of you want to help me."

He looked at her, not quite understanding, and she laughed at him. "Men," she said, and the word sounded like an oath on her lips. "Stupid, egotistical men. There never was a time when a smart woman wasn't worth a dozen of them. And you, you ride here quietly and let Monte Gordon take over the crew. Why aren't you up in front? Why aren't you fighting for your rights?"

He looked at her for a long moment in silence. His tight face muscles loosened a little, but he did not smile. "You are a spitfire, aren't you, Bantam. Well, let's hope you are as smart as you say, but I doubt it. If you were, you'd know why I ride back here. Bill is hurt. He's hurt because he took over a fight that would have been mine. Gordon and his friends have taken over, but they'll never rest easy as long as Bill is alive. If he could get up now, the crew would still probably follow him and Gordon knows it. I mean to see that Bill stays alive. Let Monte Gordon ride at the head of the column for the time. Let him think he's won. This game isn't finished yet. Gordon will have to kill me before he truly leads this crew."

XI

Monte Gordon drove them hard. All during the heat of the day they plodded forward. The sun, a ball of burning flame in the almost cloudless sky, beat down upon them without relief or mercy. And all day long the smoke signals raised their mushrooming heads toward the sky. At the brief noon halt there was some grumbling among the men that Gordon chose to ignore. Instead, he walked over to the wagon and parted the canvas that the cook had closed against the flies. He had hardly touched the cover before Andy was at his side, moving around the small fire in a dozen quick steps. Gordon heard him coming and turned, a half sneering smile parting his lips.

"You want something?"

"Leave Bill alone," Andy said.

"I wouldn't hurt him for the world," said Gordon. "I just want another look at the map."

"I have it."

"You'd better give it to me. As long as Bill is hurt, I'm leading the crew."

"Who says so?"

Tex Hart and two other men had moved up behind Gordon, the weight of their presence making itself felt. The rest of the crew watched, not taking sides, neutral until they saw what was going to happen.

"We elected him," said Tex Hart.

"I didn't." It was the cook. He had stepped to the head of the wagon and lifted down his heavy rifle that he now cradled on his arm. He did not point the gun at either Hart or the other men, but its warning was clear.

Gordon looked at him. "You'd better be careful who you pick for friends," he said.

The cook spat in the dust. "For seventy years I've been picking my friends with no help from you. I guess I'll just keep on doing it that way. As for who leads the crew, I'll listen to Bill Drake. He ain't dead yet. There's a gun beside him on the blanket in the wagon and I'll still bet he can shoot better lying down than any of you can standing on two feet."

There was a chuckle from inside the wagon and Andy realized that his brother was awake. He reached back, pulling the canvas curtains open without taking his eyes from Gordon. "You've got visitors," he told Bill.

"So I see." The elder Drake's voice was weak. His face was flushed and his lips cracked, but he managed to lift himself on his good elbow. "What's the matter Monte, getting too big for your boots?"

Even with Drake stretched out, Monte Gordon found that he had not completely lost his awe of the man. He tried to sound confident as he said: "You've got the wrong idea, Bill. I'm not trying to take over. But with you laid up, someone had to lead the crew."

"Yes, someone." Drake's irony was plain. "When I need someone to take over, I'll tell you, Monte."

Gordon looked around, feeling the need of support. The rest of the men had pressed forward when they heard Bill's voice until they formed a semicircle around the wagon's tailgate.

Only Tex Hart and two others offered Gordon real help. Tex Hart said: "Listen, Bill, we're all in this thing together and you're smashed up. These hills are full of Injuns, and they may get fuller. The sooner we locate that cached gold and hightail out of here, the healthier it'll be for all of us."

"Sure," said Bill Drake.

"And we need someone to lead us. Someone who knows the country and is on his feet."

"OK, Andy can take over."

Tex Hart breathed deeply. "No he can't." He tried to sound resolute. "I've got nothing against your brother, but he doesn't know this country and the men won't follow him."

"Meaning that they will follow Monte?"

Tex Hart's face reddened. He was not much of a talker, and he was nervous, a thing that he tried to hide. "Some of us will," he said doggedly. "I'm warning you, Bill, things are serious. None of us like the looks of the smoke that's rising from the hills. Maybe it's only a few broncos, but my guess is that there's a bigger band around somewhere, maybe Victorio. If we run into him, we need an old head and a cool one. If you insist on Andy leading, some of us will ride out, now."

Bill stirred. It was obvious that, had he been on his feet, he would have challenged Tex Hart. But he was not on his feet, and in that instant the decision was Andy's, and Andy surprised them all by saying: "He's talking a lot of sense, Bill. If we don't hang together on this, we're never going to find that gold and the chances are good that we'll never come out of these mountains. I've got no objection to taking orders from Monte."

Every one turned to look at him, and he read the condemnation in their eyes. They all realized that he had backed down. In a country where a man could not back away from a fight without losing face, he had let Monte Gordon triumph over him without even an argument. He saw that Tex Hart was sneering, that the other men were exchanging knowing glances. He felt his wounded brother's eyes upon him, he saw the unspoken disgust in the cook's face, and then he looked at Mary Thorne. She too had judged him, and thought that he was afraid. It was plain to see in her eyes. He had a sudden feeling of disgust for all of them.

Fools, he thought. It would serve them right if

he precipitated a fight that would tear the crew apart and weaken them all. If they fought now, three or four might die, and the rest would be that much weaker to face the Indians. What could the remaining ones do—turn and run for Fort Grant, praying that they reached the military post before the Indians struck? As long as they remained together, they were fairly safe. The Indians of the territory knew from bitter experience that there were many safer things to do than to attack Drake's well-trained, well-armed crew. And he had his brother to think of, the other wounded men, and, yes, damn her, the girl. For no matter how angry he grew with Mary Thorne, she was never out of his mind.

Monte Gordon cleared his throat. "I asked you for that map a while ago," he said. "I'll take it now."

Andy used his left hand to draw the map from the front of his shirt. He kept the other hand free, close to his holstered gun. "I think you're misunderstanding me," he said clearly. "Let's get it straight, Monte, once and for all. If Bill agrees, I'll follow you because we can't afford to split the crew. We'll all have to hang together if we want to live. But I won't take any of your orders unless they make sense to me, and I'm not turning this map over to you. I'm giving it back to Bill. When he says you can look at it, you can. But not before." He reached up to the wagon and dropped the folded paper at his brother's side. He heard Bill laugh and recognized the satisfaction in the sound.

"Good boy." Bill had raised himself onto one elbow. "He's right, Monte. None of us can afford the luxury of a fight right now. Here's the map." He flung it contemptuously from the wagon so that it fell at Gordon's feet. "See if you can read it. See what luck you have, and, when you get hopelessly lost, come back and talk to me."

Monte Gordon stooped slowly and picked up the folded paper. There was hate in the glance he threw at Andy. For a moment he had visualized himself making the Drakes crawl before the crew, but now the men who had not already thrown in with him were laughing at him. It was something he meant to remember. His time was coming, but for the moment he could not pick up the challenge. He spread the paper on the ground and called Tex Hart to his side. Together they traced the lines. They tried to match the map's landmarks with the country ahead, and failed. But they refused to admit their failure at once. They waited three days before they were forced to ask Bill Drake's advice.

Those three days were the most grueling that Mary Thorne could remember. The crew pressed onward, finally finding what appeared to be Superstition Mountain. Monte grudgingly asked Bill if he thought this was the Superstition. Bill concurred. They picked and entered a somewhat wider cañon in the mountainside. They made camp well inside where a muddy streak in a rocky draw indicated water, and they painstakingly dug until a small creek was exposed. Their view was restricted to narrow draws lining the peak—rocky, sinister, uninviting. After the first camp in the mountain, water grew short. Twice they made dry camps, sparingly using what was in the casks carried on the side of the swaying wagon.

It was a question now of locating the right draw, and they scouted one after another, each patrol returning more beaten out and discouraged.

Only once had they actually seen Indians, and then only in the far distance: two brown forms, outlined for a moment as they slipped over the broken rocks of a ridge top. Two of the younger riders wanted to give chase, but Monte Gordon, for all his faults, knew Apaches.

"Don't be fools," he ordered sharply. "You wouldn't have seen them unless they wanted to be seen. It's an old trick, one they've worked a hundred times . . . a trap with human bait. Those rocks are full of braves, maybe fifteen or twenty of them. If you went charging up that ridge, they'd cut you to pieces before you ever got one clean shot. They're probably after horses. Chances are they may be a band that's broken away from the agency and are on foot. Leave them alone."

The crew left them alone, but the knowledge that every movement they made was watched by unseen, hostile eyes heightened the strain under which they were already laboring.

Monte located a spring, the only real one they'd found. Here he established a kind of permanent camp, building up a brush corral for the horses and setting out regular guards, day and night. And here the brush thinned out, giving the desert grass a chance that offered forage for the stock. The rocks along the rim above were beyond rifle shot, so Indians could not slip up unseen. He was convinced that the site of the lost wagon train was somewhere within a fifteen mile radius of the camp, and he set out quartering the ground systematically, searching one cañon after another. On three separate occasions, the scouting parties had been hit by Indians who fired on them from the rocks far above without being seen. They lost three men and five horses.

Andy offered no objection to Monte's plans. For one thing, the camp offered a chance for Bill to rest, and Bill was no better. The shoulder had not responded to treatment and his big body was racked by chills and fever. His only time out of Bill's sight was to aid in the burial of the three casualties.

The cook kept the canvas sides of the wagon raised so that what little stir of air there was brought a slight relief to the wounded outlaw, but, even so, it was almost unbearable under the constant beat of the sun.

Andy stayed at Bill's side, refusing to join any of the scouting expeditions that rode out each day in a circle, searching the hundred small cañons that ran down like lacing fingers from the mountain's peak above.

They were still in brush country. It was too low for much timber, but the brush was heavy, thorny, and mean for both riders and horses. The land was so rough that at times the crew couldn't cross from one draw to the next.

At the end of the third day they gathered sullenly around the fire, rebellious and ready to quit, staring gloomily at Monte Gordon and Tex Hart who studied the map for the hundredth time.

Bill Drake lay on his wagon bunk and watched the faces of his men from under the shadow of the raised canvas side. At the moment his fever was broken and his eyes were clearer than they had been since they pulled into the camp.

Watching him, Andy felt that his brother was on the mend. Andy sat on the tailgate, idly swinging his legs, his eyes on Mary Thorne who sat on a boulder at the far side of the cooking fire. The girl had wilted visibly in the last three days. It was partly the extreme heat, partly the disappointment of having come so close and yet not finding a single trace of the treasure.

Tex Hart and Gordon were arguing over the

map, their voices rising sharply in the evening air. Andy watched and listened, only half aware of their argument. He looked up the slope, noted the two guards, motionless, outlined against the evening sky, watching out across the roughness of the country to the northwest.

"I tell you"—Hart's angry tone carried across the camp—"the cañon we're searching for has probably had a cloudburst. We've probably ridden through it, maybe more than once. My guess is, we'll never find it and we'll merely waste our time until the grub runs out. The horses have had about enough. We'd better move out of this hell-hole while we can. We shouldn't have come in the first place." He turned to stare angrily at the wagon. "We wouldn't if I'd been in command."

Bill chuckled so all the men could hear. "Have you had enough of playing leader, Monte? Are you ready for me to tell you where the gold is?"

Everyone turned in surprise. Andy noted that his brother's voice seemed stronger, that he sounded almost like his old self. The crew came slowly to their feet and pressed around the wagon.

"You mean you know?"

"Then why in hell didn't you tell us before we rode the hoofs clear off the horses?"

"Because you were acting kind of proud, Monte. I figured you needed a little lesson in discipline. I didn't start this chase blindfolded. I was up this way years ago and I found the remains of some burned wagons in a cañon over to the west. The map checks what I remembered. But I'd never heard of Mary's uncle."

New life and hope seemed to flow through the tired men. Even Gordon sounded eager. "How far from here?"

"Maybe five miles. Maybe farther the way we'll have to ride."

"Don't tell them," Andy said suddenly.

"Don't tell us what?" Monte Gordon faced around to Andy.

"Where the gold is."

The circle drew in a little, openly threatening. Even Mary Thorne roused from her lethargy and pressed forward. Gordon measured Andy. "You've been asking for trouble for a long time," Gordon said.

Bill's voice cut across his words. "You never learn anything, any of you." He mocked them from his place in the wagon. "You all should know me by this time. You should have guessed that I seldom leave anything to chance. I had a pretty fair idea of where the train burned or I wouldn't have started out. I'm not the kind of man who spends half a week searching blindly over a hundred square miles of badland."

Gordon seethed. "Why didn't you tell us sooner?"

Bill prodded him. "Monte," he said, "I told you a minute ago that you needed a lesson. I'm not sure you've learned it even yet . . . but maybe the rest of the crew have got their bellies full of your so-called leadership."

Gordon flushed darkly. Without realizing what he did, he let his hand fall toward the holstered gun at his side. Andy shifted at once, dropping to the ground and facing Gordon.

Bill said sharply: "Break it up. Neither of you has learned any sense, even now. We've got enough trouble ahead without carrying on a running fight. Stop it, both of you."

Monte Gordon managed to relax. He said in a controlled voice: "You've done a lot of talking. Now supposing you start delivering."

"All right," Bill said, and called to the cook: "Get your team up and get ready to move, Pop! I can't ride yet, but I can sit on the wagon seat. The rest of you catch horses and break camp."

They moved out at full dark, two riders on point, as scouts, in case of Indians. Bill rode propped up on the seat beside the cook, a rifle across his knees, and Andy rode beside the wagon. There was a new spirit in the crew, as if Bill's return to leadership had given them a certain confidence.

Beyond Andy, the girl paced her horse. He was extremely conscious of her, although they had not exchanged a single word for two days.

The ride stretched from five to ten to fifteen miles. The country was the roughest Andy had ever seen and it worsened steadily as they progressed.

Twice Bill ordered them to turn back and retrace a part of their route. Once he halted the chuck wagon and sat for minutes studying the mouth of a small draw that cut off to the right. And then, when the sun finally broke fully into the eastern sky, he gave a sigh of satisfaction and indicated the narrow cañon winding upward toward the distant rocky crests.

"This is it," he said.

Andy reined the horse close against the front wagon wheel. "You sure?"

Bill nodded.

Andy turned to look at the cañon. The entrance was narrow, not more than fifteen feet across, with the harsh rocky shoulders lifting sharply and widening somewhat for a distance of fifty or sixty feet above them.

"I don't like it," Andy said.

"A perfect trap," Bill agreed, pointing. "Put a man up on each rim up there, before we pull in. We can't stand being surprised in that bottleneck."

The others had gathered around, staring at the mouth of the draw. "You're certain this is the right one?" Gordon pursued.

Bill leaned forward, pointing up to a boulder that cropped out from the rim on the right like the blunted prow of a ship. "Look at the top, Monte."

The rock had been carved by the endless waves of wind and sand until it was a rough sculpture of a horse's head. The morning light, growing with each successive minute, etched it into sharp relief.

"Now look at the map."

Neither Gordon nor Andy needed to look at the map. They recalled clearly the cramped writing: **From horse-head rock, what would be about two miles looking north up the mountain.**

Gordon examined the rock. "I've ridden past here three times," he muttered. "The rock doesn't look much like a horse."

"You weren't looking at it from this angle. It's the one the map means," Bill insisted. "I remembered it from the time I found the wagons . . . and the first time I looked at the map, I spotted it."

Gordon was stubborn. "We've been up this cañon clear to the mountain. We saw no wagons."

"They were there," Bill said. "They're probably buried in the sand by now. There wasn't too much left when I saw them . . . just the wagon rims and some pieces of iron. Are you going to get flankers onto those ridges or do we sit here all day?"

Gordon shrugged and turned to give the order. Two of the horsemen started the steep ascent. They waited until these had reached the top and scanned the country, then turned and waved. Afterward, the cook started the wagon forward with the crew crowding into the narrow slot of the cañon's mouth.

It was a twisting, turning gulch, a notch torn through the barrier rock by the rushing flood waters of the past, littered with boulders, the dry stream bed shifting from one side of the cañon to the other. Old flood marks, high up on the walls, showed how the cloudbursts of other days had filled the cañon with torrents that at times had been twenty feet deep.

Andy observed them as he rode forward beside the wagon and pointed them out to his brother. "I'd hate to be caught here during a heavy rain," he said.

Bill kept his eyes on the high-water marks. His face, which had flushed during his argument at the cañon mouth, had lost its color. He looked white and drawn and tired as if the ride had drained out the last remaining segment of his strength.

Looking at him, Andy asked suddenly: "You all right?"

His brother nodded, but, a quarter of a mile farther, he told the cook to stop the wagon and had them move him back to the blanket couch in the rear.

When Andy had finished adjusting the couch, he slid out of the wagon and found Mary Thorne sitting her horse beside the trail.

"Is Bill all right?"

"What do you care?" The bitterness was plain in Andy's voice. "Bill lived up to his part of the bargain. He led you to your gold. Without him, none of us would ever have found it."

Her eyes turned dark. Without a word, she

wheeled the horse, and, driving in her spurs, she leaped it past the wagon and on up the cañon.

The cook turned to stare after her, then slowly pulled a piece of twist tobacco from his pocket and worried off a hunk with his few remaining teeth. "Son," he said in his old voice, "there goes a fine girl. Don't push her too hard."

"The hell with her," Andy said.

"You got her figured wrong," said the cook. "She's high-strung and willful and she's used to having her own way. She just got scared, that's all, finding herself lined up with this bunch of cut-throats."

Andy did not want to talk about it. "Get on with your driving, old man."

"Sure," said the cook, and climbed heavily to his high wagon seat. "I'm old and I see things different from most of you. My juices are dried up and I can look at a woman without wanting her. You can't, and Gordon can't, and most of the crew can't. They want gold, but they also want her."

Andy did not answer.

"Get her by herself," the cook told him. "Take her in your arms. That's what she wants, you young fool. I can see it in her eyes when she watches you."

Andy did not believe it. "Most of what happened is her fault," he insisted stubbornly.

The cook did not deny this. "What of it? What

difference does it make whose fault it is? I'll bet she's as sorry Bill's hurt as you are, but she'll never admit to you that she is, unless you eat your pride and make the first move."

Andy spurred on up the cañon.

The cook stared after him for a long moment, then spat, picked up the lines, and shook the team into motion. "You all right, Bill?"

Bill Drake sounded used up. "My shoulder's on fire. It's burning."

"You shouldn't have insisted on sitting up so long." Pop reached back and felt the bandage, noting the renewed bleeding. But he realized there was nothing he could do to help the wounded man, so he turned back to his driving.

Andy had already disappeared around the next bend of the twisting cañon, and the cook felt suddenly very much alone. He threw a quick glance toward the rim and was relieved to see the outline of the flanker against the sky. Still he hurried the horse as if the whole Apache nation was closing in on them from the rear.

The lumbering wagon lurched and lunged as it plowed ahead through the sand, cutting down into the river course, coming out on the other side. Three times they struck buried boulders that almost turned them over, and the horses were heaving from the pull as they came around the shoulder of the wall.

Ahead of them, a cluster of grouped horsemen

marked the crew and a long shout ran down the cañon, breathless with excitement.

"I've found it! I've found it! Here's one of the wagon tires!"

XII

Tex Hart had made the discovery. He and Monte Gordon had ridden up the cañon with the crew strung out behind them covering a good five miles before Gordon finally reined his horse in disgust.

"We've been along here twice before," he said. "We found nothing then, we're seeing nothing now, and we've certainly covered more than the two miles mentioned on the map."

Hart sat at his side, twisting in the saddle so he could look back over the trail. He studied the rock walls on either side, then once again gave his thoughtful attention to the back trail. The cañon floor rose at an angle of more than seven degrees and the stream had left its dry channel curving upward and switching from one side to the other so that they had been forced to cross it a dozen times in their upward progress. Up here it was more a wet path than a stream.

"You know," said Hart, "that wash has probably changed channel after every heavy rain."

"Of course it has."

Tex Hart went on doggedly. "Bill wasn't lying

about finding the remains of those wagons. Why should he? If he says they were in this cañon, they were. I never knew him to make a mistake about this country. He seems to be able to smell his way around where most of us get lost."

"Well?"

"Then the wagons had to be burned somewhere between here and the mouth of the cañon. The map said it was two miles. Maybe it was three, maybe it was five. Chances are the old codger wasn't too sure of his distances."

"I'm not a fool," Gordon said. "I can figure all that out for myself. Come to the point, will you?"

"Well, if the stream changed course, the chances are that, at any one time or another, it swept over the burned wagons, and any piece of wood that was left, floated away. But the iron would stay buried in the sand."

Monte Gordon was sarcastic. "If you mean we should stop and dig through all the sand from here to the cañon mouth, you're crazy. It would take all summer, even if we had the proper tools."

Hart did not answer. Instead, he turned his horse down into the bottom of the deep wash and rode back along the way they had come, his sharp eyes examining the cut banks on either side. It was thus that he found the wagon tire. It showed at the edge of the bank, buried under a good two feet of silt, only a small portion visible. He let out a small grunt of satisfaction as he swung down and climbed the bank. He worked his fingers around the edge of the rusted iron to be certain what he had, then kicked at the packed silt with his spur, loosening it until he could scoop it away with his fingers.

Gordon joined him, and the rest of the crew rode up excitedly. One of them sent back the high yell that the cook had heard. He whipped the tired horses forward, suddenly stirred by the discovery and the thought of what it might mean to him.

By the time he brought the wagon to rest, they had unearthed the tire entirely and were examining it. Bill Drake raised himself on his good elbow to peer out, and Andy held his seat in his saddle, watchful, studying each man. He saw the eager excitement in the tired faces, the rising eager greed as if the rusted iron already had turned to gold beneath their hands.

Slowly it dawned on all of them that, although they had apparently found the remains of one of the burned wagons, they had not as yet located the gold, and almost as one man they turned to look at Mary Thorne.

She, too, had remained in her saddle, motionless on the high brink of the wash's bank. Her face was streaked with dust and sweat, her eyes red-rimmed. She looked as if she might sway at any moment and tumble from her saddle.

Gordon climbed the side of the wash to where she sat, bringing with him the rusted tire as if he

were offering her proof that they had carried out their part of the bargain. He grinned up at her, the powdered dust that clung to his whiskers giving him the appearance of a dried-out reddish ghost. He held up the tire, swinging it a little in the air. He could not keep the rising note of excitement from his voice.

"We've found it, girl! We've found it, just where your uncle's map said it would be. Now it's your turn. Show us where the gold is hidden."

She hesitated for an instant, and then she glanced toward Andy as if she were wordlessly asking his permission. But there was no sign from Andy. He was not even looking at her. He was motionlessly in the saddle, one hand folded over the other on the high horn, his eyes on the wagon.

"Up there," she said, motioning to the high wall above her, "there's a kind of cave behind some rocks. My uncle said that after they stowed the gold, they rolled some boulders in to block the entrance."

They all looked at the cañon wall. It was much too steep for a horse to climb, almost too steep for a man. Rocks jutted out here and there from the barren soil, but there was no cluster such the girl described. Nevertheless, half a dozen the crew were already starting to climb, Tex in the lead, spurred on by their greed.

Their shouts came back down to the men

waited on the cañon floor, but although they quartered back and forth across the face that was so steep it would have daunted a mountain goat, their voices grew more and more discouraged.

Others, too impatient to wait, climbed to join them. Every foot of the face was examined very carefully for any sign of the blocked cave. But after almost an hour the sweaty, exhausted men gradually gave up and came sliding back down the wall. They aimed angry eyes at the girl who had dismounted and was standing at Gordon's side.

"Tell us what your uncle told you," Gordon said. "Repeat his words as exactly as you possibly can."

She wiped the back of her hand across her forehead. It was stifling hot in the cañon. The sun was almost directly overhead, beating down on them all, turning the narrow slit into a super-charged oven. She moistened her cracked lips with the tip of her tongue and said slowly, like a parrot trying to recall what had been taught him: "They were camped here, and the Indians attacked from the south rim." She pointed to the far side of the cañon. "My uncle said they managed to drive back the first attack. They held out until dark, and then decided to make a dash for it up the other wall. One of the men spotted this breastwork of rocks and pointed to it. They retreated for the rocks, each man carrying a part of the gold. They climbed under shelter of the darkness and reached the rocks, and found a little cave behind them.

They decided that, even if they broke free, they could never carry the gold out on foot, so they hid the gold in the cave and blocked its entrance as best they could. Then they climbed up over the rim and separated. After that the Indians hunted them down. Only my uncle and one other man ever showed up at Tucson."

As she talked, Gordon had been studying the cañon wall. He shook his head slowly. "There's something wrong. You say they saw rocks from here, but we can't see any."

Bill Drake had been listening from the wagon. He said now in his mocking tone: "You never try to think, do you, Monte? If facts don't seem to agree with words, you automatically think someone is lying. You're such a liar yourself, you think everyone else is always at it."

Gordon swung around. His nerves were on edge from heat and disappointment. "What are you croaking about now?"

Bill smiled. "The fact that a strong flood could well have carried that tire down the cañon from the point where it originally lay."

The whole crew turned to look at Drake, and he returned their collective stare, still grinning slightly. "So start up the cañon. We know this is the right place, and, unless someone else got here before us, the gold will still be in the cache. Somewhere along that wall between here and the mountains, there's a cave. Ride on up, watch for piles of rock, investigate each one. A thousand dollars extra to the man who finds the cave!"

Their morale, which had been at its lowest ebb, suddenly caught fire and they were gone, almost at once, mounting their horses and racing up the cañon toward the next bend. Bill watched them for a moment, then looked at his brother. Andy had not moved.

"You'd better climb to the rim," Bill said. "It would be a fine time to have Apaches move in on us while the crew is scattered from hell to breakfast."

"I'll stay with you."

Bill chuckled. "Never thought I'd see the time I needed a nursemaid. Go on, do what I tell you. I've got a rifle here and so has Pop."

Andy turned to the girl. She was still standing where Gordon had left her. He crossed to her side, saying half tauntingly: "Aren't you going to join the gold rush? You've certainly come too far to quit now."

She shrugged and walked over to where her horse was ground-hitched. She mounted, without glancing back, and rode up the cañon after the crew.

Andy watched her, frowning, then with a shrug walked over to the cañon wall and began to climb. It was too steep for a horse and he made no effort to take his mount. It was a hard ascent and it took him the better part of a ten minute struggle to reach the rim. He topped it finally and looked around.

The flanker on this side had deserted his horse and was down along the cañon side, helping in the search. Andy cursed him under his breath, guessing that Bill had suspected this and had sent him up to watch in place of the man. He walked along the crest to where the deserted animal stood dejectedly, reins trailing.

Andy caught the horse without trouble, lifted himself into the saddle, and swung around to peer across the broken land toward the mountain. It was, he judged, not more than fifteen miles to the peaks themselves. The cañon below him wound in a twisting course, swerving westward as it ran onto the flank of the mountain, breaking into a dozen shallow ravines and gullies that laced upward toward the bare rock faces of the crest.

The whole land was raw and tortured as if some massive force had reached up from below, twisting the surface into wrinkles like the skin of an old man, thrusting up rock dykes and barriers around which the flood waters of past generations had fought their way, scooping out their courses and arroyos to cut the terrain into irregular islands.

It was, he thought, perfect Indian country, offering cover in the brush for a thousand Apaches. True, the raiding bands usually numbered less than a dozen, but the Apaches had demonstrated that half a dozen of the savage warriors were the equal of a full company of cavalry.

It was not a settling thought, and Andy watched the panorama of brush and rock with careful attention. There were no smoke signals. There had been none since they had settled into their camp, which made it fairly obvious that the Indians had decided that Drake's crew had reached its destination and were waiting for something.

He had no doubt but that he was observed. He wanted to be observed, for the Apaches shared at least one characteristic with the rest of the human race. They were curious, and they might well rest quietly until they found out why these white men had thought it necessary to force their way into the dry waste of the Superstitions.

Andy hoped they would watch, but that they would not creep closer since they could see that guards were carefully posted. His main concern at the moment was to get the crew and the wagon out of the obvious trap of the narrow cañon. Once outside, he felt Drake's men could stand off any attack by the average band. If there were more of the Indians than he supposed, they would be in serious trouble.

He watched keenly, therefore, but nothing moved across the seared and twisted land save the shimmer of the heat waves as they rose from the baked ground. He kept shifting his attention, knowing full well the danger of staring too long at any given object. A man's eyes played strange tricks under the glare of the desert sun.

But for all he knew that they were in the country, he had seen no sign of where the Indians had been. They had found no deserted *rancheros*, no sign that the savages had paused to bake mescal. This, then, was probably a war party, some of Victorio's men, without women and children. As such, they could travel for miles, stripped to breechcloth and moccasins, carrying only their rifles—if they had rifles—bullet pouches, and powder. They could find water where there was none, or go eighty to a hundred miles without it. The country itself was their storehouse, although it was hard to believe that humans could find anything edible in this tumbled waste.

He looked again at the country toward the northwest, searching for any telltale sign, and then turned back, riding along the cañon rim, peering down on the wagon that the cook was driving slowly forward, and saw the girl who had returned to stay at the cook's side. From this height she looked small and slight, but, despite her weariness, she still managed to hold herself erect in the saddle, riding easily with a natural grace that was not to be mistaken.

And then a shout rose from the cañon above, and Andy spurred forward for a quarter of a mile, halting above the crew that had clustered on the hillside below him. Here the rimrock rose in a sharp granite face, a good forty feet in height. At the foot of this abrupt descent a number of fallen boulders made a kind of breastwork of the outthrust of the wall.

Andy dismounted and peered over the edge. Below him the crew was clambering across the boulders like so many ants, and he saw that they had already opened a kind of hole that slanted back into the bank. He arrived in time to see Monte Gordon disappear into the hole screened from Andy's sight by the overhang, but it was only seconds before Gordon reappeared, his hands filled with leather bags.

A thrill that he had not expected rose through Andy. Much as any man might discount his love for gold, there was still the driving compulsion about the idea of a treasure hunt. He watched Gordon disappear, to reappear with more and more pouches while the crew, their weariness forgotten, almost went crazy, jumping around the rocks and shouting, pounding each other on the back.

Finally they settled down and formed a human chain, passing the bags down to the wagon on the cañon floor. Not until the last bag had arrived safely did the guard, who had deserted his post on the cañon rim, remember his duty and look upward. He saw Andy on his horse and waved. Andy motioned to him and the man climbed reluctantly, reaching Andy's side red-faced and

puffing. But his excitement outweighed everything else.

"Never saw so much gold in my life." He was
babbling. "Big as corn kernels. Millions of
nuggets."

Andy dismounted, saying harshly: "You leave
your post again and Bill will have to shoot you, if
the Apaches don't get you first. Now keep your
eyes trained. We have the gold and we certainly
don't want to lose it to the Indians. Or lose our
hair, either."

He left the man muttering to himself and slid
down the steep wall, almost falling in his descent.
Around him the crew was in turmoil. Someone
had spread a piece of canvas on the ground beside
the wagon, and on this Monte Gordon had
emptied part of one of the pouches. The gold
looked like course sand, water-worn from its
contact with the rough gravel of some ancient
streambed farther up the mountain. It was dullish,
rather than bright and shining as Andy had
expected. He had never before seen placer gold—
rusty gold as it was sometimes called because of a
thin coating from oxidation that covered the soft
metal like a scum. He stood to one side, watching
the excited men as one after another let the coarse
nuggets run through scarred fingers. Then he
looked around to see Bill Drake's lips, but the
smile did not reach his pain-shadowed eyes.

Mary Thorne was taking no part in the

celebration. She sat on a rock, withdrawn, out of the central picture as if she were a spectator witnessing something that she did not quite understand.

Bill saw Andy's questioning look and motioned him over to the wagon. "Let them have their fun," he said in an undertone. "They've worked hard enough in the last few days."

"We'd better pull out of here," Andy said. "The longer we stay in this cañon, the longer we're sitting in a trap. I don't like it. We don't want to lose the gold the same way that the men did who first dug it."

His brother's eyes were extra bright from fever, but they came into sharp focus at Andy's words. "See any sign up there?"

Andy shook his head. "That's what worries me. I saw no sign, yet we know they're around here somewhere, watching us. We'd better hope it isn't Victorio."

"It isn't," said Bill. "At least the ones that jumped us weren't his main party. If they had been, we'd probably be dead by now. It was a small bunch, maybe not even Chiricahuas. Just some broncos looking for horses."

"Still, I wouldn't want to be caught in this cañon. With Indians on those rims we'd be dead before we fought our way half the distance toward the mouth. Let's get out of here before sundown."

Bill nodded, straightened out a little, and raised

his voice. "All right! You've all had your fun, now it's time to ride if you ever expect to spend that gold. Let's get the wagon turned, the dust loaded, and start back toward water."

The crew turned. Monte Gordon rose slowly to his feet and came through their split ranks until he faced the Drakes. "We haven't talked yet about how the gold gets split."

Bill showed impatience. "There's a time and a place for everything, Monte. Let's get it safely out of the country first. Then we can argue about the split."

Gordon glanced around at the other men, and there was something in the way they returned Gordon's look that Andy did not like. But to his surprise, they offered no further protest. They gathered up the leather pouches and loaded them into the wagon, then went after their horses. They motioned to the flankers above, turned back down the cañon. But not until the last rider was free of the narrow jaws, coming out onto the flatland beyond, did Andy draw a deep breath of relief.

XIII

That night there was an air of festival. They had come back to their camping grounds, turning the tired horses into the brush corral after watering them thoroughly. Andy had ridden guard behind the wagon during the march from the cañon, content to eat the swirling dust as he covered the retreat.

But before they had covered half the distance, he was surprised when Mary Thorne reined her horse back and fell in at his side. He glanced at her twice, waiting for her to speak, but for the moment she made no attempt to talk to him. She rode slowly forward, apparently wrapped in her own thoughts, and, from her expression, he judged that they were far from pleasant.

Finally Andy could stand it no longer and said sarcastically: "I'm surprised that you aren't riding next to the wagon, keeping a careful eyes on your beloved gold."

She turned on him, and her eyes were dark with anger. "I wish I'd never heard of it, or you," she said.

Andy's jaw slackened. For a moment he did not know what to say. Then his humor rallied. "Bantam," he told her, "I've always heard women were changeable, but you take all the prizes. First, you come bustling out here as if your clothes are on fire. Nothing will do but that you must go after this gold. Then we find it, after riding through hell to get here, and now you say you hate it."

"I do." Her voice was passionate. "I hate it. I wish I'd never heard of it. I wish I'd never come into this country."

He stared at her for a long moment, then let his eyes wander ahead to the string of riders. These men were hardened outlaws, calloused by years upon the frontier, but now they acted like schoolboys just released for an unexpected vacation.

"You wouldn't find many in this outfit to agree with you," he told her. "I never saw them so happy and relaxed. To hear them, you'd think that they were almost human."

She glanced sidewise at him, and her tone changed. "You have a bitter tongue, Andy Drake."

"I do," he admitted.

"And a bitter mind," she said. "I never troubled to tell you why I needed this gold, why I had to have it, why it represented my last chance."

He was unbending, not seeking her confidence, giving her no help. "People all have troubles." He sounded indifferent. "And I've found, watching them, that most people think their troubles are more important than anything that's happening to someone else."

"Meaning you think your troubles are greater than mine."

The look he threw at her was one of genuine surprise. "I didn't mention that I had any trouble to speak of. In fact, I guess I don't. A man has to own things to have real trouble. He's got to have people depending on him. I have nothing like that and no one who cares whether I live or die."

"What about your brother?"

"Bill?"

"Of course, Bill. Aren't you worried about him? He's not in good shape, you know. It's only that iron will of his that keeps him going."

Andy softened a little as he said slowly: "I'll tell you something I've discovered about Bill and me. That night outside of Tucson, for instance. I hated him then as much as you did, maybe more. I was his brother and I felt a certain responsibility for the things he did." He stopped, waiting for her to respond, but she was not looking at him. She was staring ahead at the tailgate of the moving wagon, and he noticed that her lips had curved a little, that she was almost smiling. Suddenly he became suspicious. *We aren't quarreling,* he thought. *For the first time in days we're speaking to each other civilly like ordinary people. There's something the matter. She wants me to do something. She's buttering up to me the way she did Gordon, the way she did the rest of that crowd. I'll watch her. I'll play her game, but she won't take me in.*

He managed to keep his voice level as he went on. "I resented Bill ever since I had joined the crew. I resented him like a kid brother, like a boy without too much sense. And I kept on resenting him until he stepped in and took over my fight with the Pecos Kid."

"And now?"

"Bill hasn't changed," Andy said. "Maybe it's me that's changed. But I understand him better

206

than I did. He's still exactly what he was. He makes no pretense of being anything else. I think that's where he gets his strength, that and his lack of fear. He'll die sometime, probably from a bullet. I hope he does. I have no desire to see him at the end of a rope. But I don't want to see him die here, either. Because if he does, it will be from the hurt he took, fighting for me."

"No," she said. "He was hurt because of me. I don't want to see him die for the same reason."

Andy looked at her again, almost believing, yet not quite daring to. This girl had hurt him before and he did not mean to leave himself open to be hurt by her again.

But she went on, ignoring his look. "That's why I'm talking to you now. It was my fault, and it will be my fault if he's killed."

"Killed?"

"By Gordon," she said. "I made a deal with Gordon. Once the gold was found, he was to take over the crew, standing against your brother. But when I planned it, Bill hadn't been hurt. He wasn't crippled. I don't fight a crippled man when he's powerless to defend himself."

Andy stared at her. Suddenly his mind was twisted again by the suspicion that he knew why she was doing this. She had not changed. She was as tricky as ever. She had made a deal with Gordon in order to fight Bill Drake, but now that Drake was hurt and no longer a threat to her, she feared Gordon more than she feared Bill. So now she was appealing to Andy, working on him, setting him up to fight her battle with Gordon, perhaps kill Gordon. His mouth tightened grimly. All right, he would fight Gordon. He had intended to from almost the first, but he would wait until they were all safely out of the Indian country.

He knew now that Bill had been entirely right about women. They were a conniving lot, scheming and planning until no man was safe anywhere within sight of them. *She was,* he thought, *like one of the trap-door spiders, weaving her web and entangling the whole crew in its silky strands.* Nothing would serve her better than if they all killed each other, leaving her alone to enjoy the full value of the recovered gold. If she could reach Fort Grant or Tucson, he had no doubt that she would turn on all of them. "It's not going to work," he said aloud.

She looked around, startled. "What are you talking about?"

"You," he said. "You with your pretty face that should belong to an angel. You've worked every-thing out very carefully, haven't you? And things are turning out about the way you planned. You must have been born under a lucky star, Bantam."

"What *are* you talking about?"

"You know what I'm talking about," he said. "You got to Gordon, and through Gordon you got to the Kid, and the Kid winged Bill. Now, if your luck holds, Gordon and I will kill each other and your plans will all have worked out fine. . . ."

She was staring at him, too stunned for the moment to speak. All afternoon she had nerved herself for this interview, crowding down her pride, ready to tell Andy she was sorry for all that had happened, to tell him his life was in grave danger from Gordon and Tex Hart, for she had overheard the two men talking together after the gold had been found. But at Andy's scathing words a blinding rage rose up to wipe everything else from her mind so that it was impossible for her suddenly stiff lips to form the proper words.

"You . . . ," she managed to gasp. "You blind, ignorant fool!" Then finding it impossible to say more, she drove her spurs into her startled horse and the frightened animal plunged down the trail after the wagon. Mary Thorne had never been so angry with anyone in her whole life. She told herself that Andy was even worse than his murdering brother. At least, Bill Drake did not go around judging people and their motives. She had only wanted to help. She owed him nothing, nothing at all. She owed none of them anything, and at the moment she would cheerfully see them all hanged for the thieves and killers that they were. She shuddered to think that she had ever gotten involved with any of them. That had been her first mistake, to seek out Drake and his crew of cut-throats. But in this she had acted solely on

Wakeman's advice, and she had had no reason to question the lawyer's honesty. Two tears squeezed their way out from under her sunburned lids. She shook her head, sniffling to check the sobs. What in the devil was the matter with her anyway? She was not the crying type. She could hardly remember a time that she had cried, and certainly Andy Drake was not worth shedding tears about. She assured herself that she had no interest in what would happen to him. Now she meant to get back to Tucson as quickly as possible, to take her share of the gold, and return home. The chances were good that she and Andy would never meet again. She would be rid of him, and, if Gordon failed to kill him, someone else would. She thought she should find some comfort in the thought, but she found none.

And that raised the question of Gordon. What was she going to do about Monte Gordon? He would undoubtedly demand his reward, now that the gold was found, now that they had it safe. But was it safe? They weren't out of the badlands. They must be 100 miles from Fort Grant, much farther than that from Tucson, and the ranches that had once dotted this country were gone, burned out by Victorio's raids.

She glanced around half fearfully, realizing that she had entirely forgotten the danger from the Indians. She wondered if the rest of the crew were as careless. But although she searched the broken country to right and left, there was nothing to arouse her suspicion. She relaxed, staring ahead at the lumbering wagon with its 200 pounds of gold, at Monte Gordon and Tex Hart who were riding beside it as if they did not dare to get too far away from the treasure. The sight of them brought her mind back with a rush to the tangled maze of her own problems, and she had a smothered sensation as if there were no possible hope of escape.

So she rode on as the sun sank, almost dreading the time that they would reach the camp for fear that she would be called upon to make a final decision that night. But after the camp was reached, no one paid too much attention to her. The men were still in high good humor, and from somewhere Monte Gordon had dug up a bottle of trade whiskey that went the rounds, passing from hand to hand. There was not enough to turn the men sullen or dangerous, merely enough to hold the biting edge of their good humor.

Mary Thorne sat and watched the gaiety, feeling more alone and friendless than she had ever felt in her whole life. But she was not so involved in her own misery that she failed to notice two things. First, Andy was not included in the rejoicing. The bottle had not been offered to him. It was a small thing, almost meaningless in itself, and she could not be certain that it was not merely a careless oversight, or due to the fact that he had not joined the group around the fire but ate, sitting on the wagon tailboard talking to his brother. It did set him apart from the others, and she saw that Gordon, for all his seeming carelessness, watched the younger Drake as if hoping that Andy would make an issue of the apparent slight. Andy took no notice of this, but he did make an issue of something else when Gordon and Hart rose and moved over to the wagon.

"It's your turn to guard the horses," Gordon said. "Get your mount and drift out west. We don't want the war whoops crowding us tonight."

Andy slid from the tailgate. "Don't push me, Monte." His tone was mild, but his eyes weren't. There was a wicked eagerness that showed that he actually would welcome a fight.

But Gordon was deceptively friendly. "I'm not crowding you, Andy. We've gotten what we came for. There's not need of us quarreling now. Let's forget the past."

"Sure," Andy said. "So don't push me."

Gordon tried to mask his impatience. "I tell you I'm not pushing you. We've got to keep a guard and we've all got to take our turn."

"Take yours then. I'm not leaving this camp tonight."

"If that's the way you feel . . ."

"That," Andy said, "is exactly the way I feel."

Gordon repeated his shrug. He hesitated for a moment longer, then turned and went back to the fire. He ordered two of the other men out on guard, and then came toward the wagon. Andy had not moved.

"Any objection if we have another look at the gold?" The question was mocking.

Andy ignored the taunt. He stood aside so Gordon could crawl into the wagon and watched while Monte passed out the leather sacks, one after another. The men carried them to the blanket beside the fire, gathering around like eager children amused by new toys.

"Look at them." It was Bill Drake, peering out over the edge of the wagon box. "Tonight every one of them thinks he's a millionaire."

Andy did not answer. He watched the group by the fire, and then glanced at the silent girl, sitting huddled and alone beyond the blaze. Then his attention went back to the men and he said softly, thinking aloud: "If they had a couple more bottles of whiskey, they'd be cutting each other's throats within the hour. I'm sorry they haven't got it."

Bill glanced at him. The fever flush had faded from his cheeks leaving them gray and sunken under his heavy tan. "What's wrong with you now? The girl again?"

"She's no good," Andy said. "She made a deal with Gordon. This afternoon she warned me, thinking I'd kill him and thereby get her out of it."

"You could do worse." Bill turned appraising eyes toward the still figure. "She's something to look at and she has a spirit."

"And she's crooked as hell."

Bill was silent, considering, and Andy added: "You know, Gordon plans to get rid of us before we reach Tucson."

Bill's laugh was cynical. "Everyone in the territory will give him a vote of thanks."

"But he won't get away with it," Andy said. "I'll kill him first. I'd have killed him before now if we didn't need him to help hold off the Indians." He turned then, not wanting more talk, and walked away to sit down with his back to a rock, pulling his hat down so that it shadowed his eyes. He needed sleep badly. Everyone in the crew needed sleep, but Andy had hardly closed his eyes since his brother had been hurt, and he had no intention of sleeping now. He sat and watched the camp. He watched the cook cross over to the wagon and gently as a woman fix Bill's blankets for the night. He saw the crew tire of playing with the gold and carry it back to be stowed under the high seat. He saw the guards ride in and other men go out to take their places. Gradually the crew settled down for the night, circled about the embers of the dying fire.

He had dozed. He came awake, conscious of the early morning chill eating through him, stiffening his muscles. He shifted to restore his lagging circulation and suddenly was aware that two men were standing over him. He started to get up, his hand falling naturally toward the holstered gun.

Tex Hart's voice stopped him. Tex Hart was holding a rifle, its frowning muzzle not over two feet from Andy's chest. Tex Hart said: "Don't try it, Drake. I'd just love to plug you."

Andy realized that the man was laughing down at him, thoroughly pleased. He stopped, knowing that this was not a bluff, that Hart meant exactly what he said.

Slowly Hart took a step backward and ordered him to rise. He came up and turned his back in obedience to the command, and knew it was Monte Gordon's touch as the man's hand lifted the gun from his holster. He turned then, saying in a half-strangled voice: "What's this?"

"This," said Gordon, "is the end for you."

Andy's brain was sharp and clear now and no longer drugged from sleep. "So you've lost your nerve. You don't think you could beat me."

Monte Gordon chuckled. "You can't bait me into fighting, Andy." He sounded almost friendly. "I promised her you wouldn't be hurt."

For a moment Andy failed to understand. Then he said slowly: "You promised her you wouldn't kill me?"

"Yes." Monte Gordon smirked. "She doesn't want to marry a murderer. She said that if I killed you and your brother, she wouldn't have anything more to do with me."

"Nice of her," Andy said. "And just what do you plan to do with us?"

Gordon chuckled. "Leave you here. We won't hurt you at all. We'll just tie you up alongside the spring. We'll leave some food . . . but we won't leave any guns or horses."

Andy sickened as the meaning of the man's words soaked into his mind. He knew now why Gordon was in such good humor. Even if he and Bill managed to survive hunger and thirst, they could hardly hope to walk out of this hostile Indian country. With Bill wounded and weak, they would never make it.

Gordon and Hart were going to tie him up. Would they also tie up his brother? He wondered how much of this plan the girl understood. Maybe the whole thing was her idea, a way of ridding herself of the Drakes without actually having their blood on her hands. A black rage filled him. Without warning he charged Monte Gordon, heedless of the rifle Tex Hart held. If he were going to die, Hart's rifle bullet would be far more merciful than thirst, starvation, or spread-eagled torture across an ant hill to provide entertainment for the Apaches.

Gordon was not prepared for the rush. He tried to step aside, but Andy was already on top of him. His swinging fist caught Gordon high on the cheek bone, splitting the skin and knocking the man from his feet. Andy jumped on him. He reached for his own gun that Gordon had thrust carelessly into his belt. But he never had a chance.

Tex Hart stepped in, swinging the heavy rifle barrel like a club. Tex brought it down across the back of Andy's head.

Andy went over onto his face without a sound. Monte Gordon wiggled out from under his big body and climbed slowly to his feet. He stood for an instant, staring down at the prostrate man. His face twisted with rage. Then he kicked Andy in the side.

"Tie him up and let's get moving," Gordon said.

Mary Thorne came around the wagon. Her voice was only a shadowed whisper. "If you've killed him . . ."

"Worse luck we didn't," Monte Gordon said. "He has a head like a boulder. Tie him up, Tex, get Bill out of that wagon. We've got to roll."

Mary Thorne moved over to Gordon's side and stood looking down at the unconscious Andy. "Why do you need to tie him up?"

Monte grinned at her. "Give him something to think of when he comes to. Go ahead, Tex."

Tex Hart bent to his task with a will. Andy knew nothing about it. His first hazy remembrance came almost an hour later. He stirred then, trying to sit up, and failing. Both wrists and ankles were fastened. Tex Hart had passed a rope through the bonds and tightened it so that Andy lay in a semi-crouched position that did not even allow him to roll over. He lay on his side, faced away from the camp. He could hear the stir of the men and horses, the voice of the cook as he raised it to shout at the team, then the *creak* of the dry wagon wheel as the outfit began to move.

He lay listening. Already the sun had climbed above the eastern mountains but was not yet high enough to have much warmth. It would get hotter as the day progressed, many times hotter, and he wondered how long he would stay sane, lying there exposed to its full glare. A man could not take too much sun in this country, especially with no water.

He lay quietly, listening to the sound of hoofs and the wagon as they died in the distance. Then he heard a light noise behind him and knew a quick stab of fear.

"Who is it?"

The voice brought reassurance. "Me," said Bill.

Andy almost cried out of relief. His first thought had been of Indians, savages creeping up on the deserted camp. He had for the moment forgotten Bill's very existence.

"You tied up, too?"

"I was." The sardonic note rang clear in Bill's voice. "They tied me, but Pop slipped over to give me one last drink of water. Good old cookie. He had a knife under his coat and he had time for one slash. My arms are free."

"Come get me loose."

"I'm coming," Bill said.

It seemed to Andy that it took Bill an extremely

long time and he could not understand the delay until his brother worked around into his view. Bill had the knife clenched in his teeth. He was sitting upright, edging himself forward with the aid of his unbroken arm. His useless one hung in the sling at his side, the shoulder bandage showing red from fresh blood as if the wound had again broken open. His face was gray from his efforts. A white circle showed around his tightly pressed lips and there were beads of moisture across the forehead. He was in deep pain, but he moved on until he could reach Andy's bonds with the knife blade. He drew it quickly across the leather thongs, and Andy felt the bonds loosen. His hands were free now, but they were so deadened from the lack of circulation that it was all he could do to move his fingers.

Returning blood brought its sharp pain, its tingling pins and needles. Minutes passed before he could control his hands properly. Then he used the knife to free his ankles and stood up, looking around at the litter of the abandoned camp. Finally he felt his head. It ached dully when he touched a long egg-sized welt behind one ear.

The departing crew had left very little of value. There was a small store of dried food and a single water bottle. Considering the food, Andy wondered if Gordon had been indulging in a macabre sense of humor when he tied them up, yet left food and water that they could not hope to reach. Then

Andy realized that the food and water bottle probably had been placed there to impress Mary Thorne with Gordon's kind-heartedness. Perhaps the girl had been told that their bonds were so loose that they could work out of them. No matter what Gordon's motive was or what the girl had thought, they didn't count now.

He went over to Bill, gathered him in his arms, and carried him to the spring. Bill had lost weight in the last few days, but he was still too heavy to carry very far. As Andy put him down in the sand beside the water, Bill looked up at his brother.

"Don't try it," he said.

"Try what?"

"To get me out of here. Alone you've got one chance in a thousand to walk out to Fort Grant. With me, you'd never make ten miles. Leave me here, at the spring, with a little jerky. You take the rest of the grub and the water bottle. When it gets hot, hole up until the evening. If you make the fort, you can send back for me."

"The Indians will find you first."

Bill Drake shrugged and his voice echoed the fatalism that had ruled his life. This was the end of the road. He knew it. He knew that it was useless to struggle, so he didn't pretend.

"Leave me the knife," he said. "If the red devils show up, I'll use it before they can get me. As for you, get to the fort. Then track down Monte Gordon and cut out the bastard's guts." The first trace of hate showed in Bill's eyes. "I wouldn't have cared if he'd killed us. In his spot, I'd have done the same thing. But to leave us for buzzard bait, knowing that the hills are full of Apaches . . ." He broke off, lacking words to vent his feelings.

Besides, Andy had stopped listening. Andy was studying the rocks, the bare landscape that unfolded in creased rolls, rising steadily toward the distant peaks. "We've got to get out of here," he said. "We've got to find a place to hide." He filled the water bottle at the spring and offered it to Bill. He took his own drink and refilled the bottle. Then he packed the dried food carefully, making a small bundle that he slung over his shoulder. Next, despite his brother's continued protests, he lifted Bill to his shoulder, and moved away. He covered his tracks as best he could, stepping in the wagon marks as far as the small creek and then following it downward until it curved around a jutting rock shoulder. There he paused to rest.

Afterward he began to climb up the shoulder toward a mass of scattered rocks 200 feet above. It was hard work, with the heat increasing, and twice he slipped, almost plunging Bill and himself into the stream bed below. But somehow he reached the goal, a small sandy patch of almost level ground entirely surrounded by boulders bigger than a man. Above them the rocks climbed sharply, overhanging near the crest creating protection from above. Bill and Andy were fairly concealed from the crest. The spot was far from perfect, and they were still much too close to the abandoned camp ground to please Andy, but it was the best he could do at the moment.

He made his brother as comfortable as possible, digging hip holes in the packed sand. Then he stripped off the dirty bandage and examined the wound. It was angry red and lined with proud flesh. It made Andy a bit ill, but he tried to be cheerful.

"We're not done yet," he told Bill.

"Ha!" Bill tried to grin and made a poor attempt of it. The climb up the cañon side had hurt him badly. "You're all right, kid. You'll do to ride with. But what's the use of fooling yourself? You aren't by any chance expecting a stagecoach to come along and pick us up, are you?"

Andy kept his smile in place. "You never know."

Bill shook his head. "Go on. Strike out for the fort while you still have a chance. You can send back for me."

"And you'd be dead before help ever came. That water bottle wouldn't last you two days." Andy busied himself smoothing out a place in the sand, preparing to lie down.

Bill's voice was gruff. "You know, kid, we wouldn't be in this mess, if I'd thought a little before I killed Wakeman."

Andy froze, his hands spread in the sand. His words were barely audible. "Why did you?"

"He made it pretty clear we didn't need to share with the girl. She'd obviously trusted him about the map. I've never taken to killing women. I mean it, kid, you better get going . . . you can send back for me."

Andy took a deep breath. "You'd be dead long before that."

"All right, I'd be dead then. But I'd die happy knowing that, if you got through, you'd take care of that bastard Gordon."

"We'll see," said Andy gruffly, unable to say more. A long moment passed. "Get some rest. We'll decide later. It's too hot to start now, anyhow." He settled back, finding what shade he could, and closed his eyes. But it grew hotter and hotter in the rocks, the waves beating off the granite surfaces, reflecting down upon them as if they had been crowded into an oven.

And suddenly there were sounds from the abandoned camp below. Andy had not seen them come, his eyes closed against the glare. He opened them, stretched, then peered down and stiffened as he counted seven Apaches prowling around the ashes of the dead fire. He watched them, tense and motionless, unconsciously gripping the handle of the small knife that protruded from his belt. It wasn't much of a weapon, but it was all he had.

XIV

Andy couldn't remember how long he had crouched there in the rocks, watching the Indians examine the camp below. He realized that they must have come over the far rim, and there was no sign of horses. Perhaps they had left their horses back in the hills, suspecting a trap. He had no way of knowing, but they were going over the ruins of the camp thoroughly, motioning to each other, apparently not suspecting that they were observed.

Bill groaned in his sleep, and Andy put a warning hand over his brother's mouth.

Bill awoke instantly, eyes staring up into Andy's face, lips forming the soundless words: "What is it?"

"Apaches, seven of them, in the old camp."

Bill managed to sit up, to have his cautious look around one of the sheltering rocks. "If they ever find your tracks, we're goners."

"They haven't looked yet," Andy said. "They must think everyone pulled out."

"You'd better hope they keep thinking so."

Apparently they did. They looked at the trail made by the horses and wagon, and gestured among themselves. But they did not follow it to the creek, and therefore did not find Andy's sign.

Instead, they left the way they had come, up over the far rim, vanishing into the brush and rocks as if by magic.

"Thank God," Andy said, and sighed with relief.

"Don't be so sure." Bill was watching the distant hillside and the rocks beyond. "Those bucks may have horses somewhere, and possibly a few more men. I couldn't tell what tribe from this distance, but we're lucky if that's the last we see of them. They may have spotted us. If so, they'll be circling to close in from behind."

Andy shrugged. There was nothing he could do, but, as the day wore on and there was no more sign of the hostiles, he breathed easier. The sun slanted down now, and there was a stir of air coming up the cañon so that it was markedly cooler. He gave his brother a drink and had a small sip for himself. The water was warm, tasting almost brackish from the bottle. He shook it, surprised at how very little remained.

"As soon as it's full dark, I'll slip down and get a reload," he said. He dug some jerky from the pack and passed it to Bill. The wounded man tried to eat and failed. His face was more drawn now, his eyes feverish. Andy watched him with concern, not knowing what to do. It was obvious even to his untutored eyes that Bill had gotten worse.

Andy was conscious of a deep-rooted anxiety and this surprised him. He and his brother were

225

little more than strangers. He had never seen eye to eye with Bill since he had joined the crew. At times, he recalled, he actually had wished his brother dead. But Bill's admission about Wakeman had hit him hard. He'd already learned that his brother didn't kill without thinking it necessary. He had buried the fact about Wakeman. Now his jaw was set—determined. It if were humanly possible, he meant to carry Bill out. At dark he would go down to the thread-like stream and fill the water bottle, then he would rig a sling with the blanket and get Bill onto his back so that he would have his hands free.

They would not try to follow the route the crew had taken out of the valley. That way, they were bound to leave a trail that the Indians undoubtedly would pick up. He meant, instead, to swing eastward across the broken hills, resting by day, traveling by night. It was their only chance to reach Fort Grant with its surgeon.

He did not tell Bill. That would only provoke useless argument. He sat there, waiting for darkness. Under its blanketing shadow he took the water bottle and slipped over the rock barrier. He made his way down the slope without incident. He had filled the bottle and was bending down for a long drink when a yell lifted him upright.

The yell was high-pitched, eerie, without words. But it was Bill's voice, warning him. Andy knew at once what the warning meant. Nothing could make Bill break the silence unless Indians had crept back and were attacking.

He turned then, gripping the cook's knife, and moved quickly yet silently up the rocks. Even as he climbed, he knew it was a foolish thing to do. If the Indians were there, his brother probably had died yelling. By climbing, he was merely placing himself in a deathtrap.

Yet he climbed, keeping as close to the rising ground as he could so they would not spot him among the shadows.

Above him he heard a series of grunts. Then he heard them talking and knew that there was more than one. For an instant he paused, breathing slowly and deeply yet silently. He listened, trying to judge.

Apparently they thought that Bill was alone. He did not know what they thought; he would never know. But suddenly above him a fire flickered, and through the rocks he had a single glimpse of his brother. Bill was still alive.

Andy saw him propped up against a rock, glaring up at his captors, uncowed and unafraid. They crouched before him, baiting him. And they were so engaged with the pleasure of their task that they did not detect Andy until he mounted the circle of rocks. He stood there for an instant, knife hand raised. Then he leaped, landing behind the nearest brave. His left arm crooked about the man's throat, dragging his head backward as he drove the knife deeply into the man's side just under the armpit. The knife came up again and he struck a second time, so rapidly that the brave had not even the time to drop his rifle. Andy wrenched it from his grasp as he fell. He twisted it around with one hand, rested the stock against his hip, and fired directly into the chest of the second Indian.

The very restricted space interfered with his opponents. They had no room to strike at him because of their own men. Andy flung away the empty gun as the third Indian jumped at him, but Bill Drake had heaved himself erect. Bill leaned backward against a boulder for support. His good hand came out to seize the Apache's greasy hair and jerk the man back against him. He held the brave thus for the split second that Andy needed to stab him twice.

But even as Andy stabbed, the fourth Indian shot Bill Drake directly behind the ear. Bill swayed for an instant, his body trying instinctively to steady itself even though he was already dead. Then he fell forward, carrying the Indian that Andy had just stabbed to the ground under him.

The remaining Indian's gun was empty, but he still had his axe. With a muted yell, he dropped the gun and sprang toward Andy. Andy dropped to one knee, catching up the rifle he had let fall. He saw the axe blow coming and raised the barrel just in time to catch the downswing of the blade. It struck the metal with a force that almost tore the rifle from his grasp. But the handle turned in the Indian's hand and slid down the metal of the barrel, striking Andy's forearm a glancing blow.

The arm was cut clear to the bone, but if it had not been for the gun barrel, the arm would have been entirely severed. Andy went to one knee, but with his other hand he struck upward, a stabbing, slashing rip, his knife blade entering at the Indian's groin and opening the stomach wide, as neatly as if a surgeon had aimed the blow. For an instant the Indian stood, almost disemboweled, trying to lift his axe by the very force of his will. Then he crumpled, folding rather than falling, until he dropped across Bill Drake's lifeless body.

Andy stared around him, still on his knees, hardly believing that the four savages were dead. He drew a long shuddering breath, and then stared vacantly at the blood welling from the cut in his useless arm.

Reason came back to him, and he rose unsteadily. He stooped, tore away what remained of Bill's ragged shirt, and rigged a tourniquet to stop the flow of spurting blood. Then he leaned against the rock, feeling sick, dizzy, and washed out.

Minutes passed before he had the strength to rig a bandage over the cut itself. The whole lower part of the forearm was numb. Later, pain would start, but now the flesh had almost no feeling. But he had no time to worry about the arm. There had been seven Apaches searching the camp that morning. Four were with him here, dead. Where were the other three?

There might be more, of course, many more. He had no way of knowing. But every minute he remained where he was increased the danger that he might be discovered. He stooped, caught up the axe that had almost severed his arm, and thrust the short shaft through his belt. He selected the best of the Indian guns, loaded it from a brave's bullet pouch, and put the pouch in his pocket. Afterward he slid down to where he had dropped the water bottle, refilled it, and drank deeply from the creek. Then he began climbing again, past the circle of the rocks, and up over the rim.

Fifteen minutes later he found the horses, picketed in a small draw. He watched them in the gathering light from the distant moon, trying to make certain that there was no guard. He saw no one and finally stole forward.

The animals were gaunt from hard riding, from little food and less water. An Apache seldom took care of a horse, especially on a raiding party. They were usually ridden into the ground and replacements stolen. Often the worn-out animals were killed and eaten as well.

There were no saddles and the bridles were only rope, twisted into a kind of hackamore. He took the horse that seemed in the best shape and turned the others loose. He would have liked to take an extra horse with him, but it would only double the chance that the Indians might spot him. It was hard to mount without the aid of stirrups, with his injured arm, and with the Indian rifle in his good hand. But he made it finally. The horse was too weary to give him much trouble, and he turned the animal southeast, heading across some of the roughest country he had ever seen.

He had only one purpose in mind, to catch up with the crew and deal with Monte Gordon. But he did not hurry. He rode cautiously, keeping as much as possible in the darker shadows, examining each small section of country before crossing it.

His arm had begun to throb, a sharp, pounding pain that made him dizzy and dulled his senses. He rode on, fighting the desire to halt, to lie down, to sleep. He had to keep on. He was roughly paralleling the route that Gordon and the crew had taken, but, where they had stayed in the cañons, pulling around the jutting hills, he cut directly across the rugged country. If the Indians were trailing the crew, they were much less apt to pick up his sign, but now and then he cut down into the lower country, checking the tracks of the riders and the wheel marks left by the wagon.

In this maze of hills a man could well lose his own way, and it would have been easy for him to miss the crew entirely. Each time he checked the wagon tracks, he looked carefully for Indian sign, but saw none. He was getting a little careless as he crossed a stony ridge and dropped down the next draw into the main cañon. Suddenly his horse nickered, and a sharp challenge came out of the darkness below him.

"Hold up, there! Sing out, quick!"

Andy almost fell from his horse as he recognized the cook's voice, but he managed to call: "It's me . . . Andy."

"Well I'll be damned." Pop came slowly out of the deep shadows, carrying his heavy rifle, throwing a dozen questions at Andy as he came. "How'd you get here? Where's Bill . . . ?"

But as Andy swung down heavily from his horse, Mary Thorne brushed by the cook.

"Andy, you're here? You're all right?" She had both arms around his neck before he realized what she was about. She held him closely as if she were afraid that he might vanish into the night, and suddenly he realized that she was crying.

He dropped the rifle and his good arm tightened convulsively around her slim body. "Why, Bantam . . . I . . ."

She raised her face and pressed her mouth against his. Her lips were parted and hot and the tip of her tongue was searching. "Oh, Andy," she drew back a little, whispering, "I'm a fool. I don't care if I'm making a fool of myself. I thought I'd never see you again. I almost died while Gordon was tying you up. I . . ." She was suddenly conscious of his injured arm. "Andy, what is it? What's happened to you?"

"Apaches." The word fell between them like a knife, and for a moment neither the girl nor the cook said anything.

Finally Mary Thorne asked in a small voice: "What happened?"

Andy told them. He did not elaborate on the fight, or on Bill's death. He told them quietly, and then he told them about finding the horses and riding southeastward.

The cook said slowly: "And no horse guards?"

He shook his head. "I didn't see any."

Mary Thorne had recovered some of her composure, and her tone was almost business-like as she said: "Let me look at that arm."

"It's all right," Andy assured her, ignoring the throbbing. "I spoiled his aim with the rifle barrel. Otherwise, he would have cut it off."

She wouldn't listen. She took off the bandage and examined the cut, making little sounds of sympathy as she did so.

Andy looked across her bent head at the watching cook. "How do you two happen to be here alone? Where's the rest of the crew?"

The girl answered. She said in a low voice without lifting her eyes to his face: "As soon as I saw you lying there unconscious, I knew I'd been wrong, but I didn't dare protest too much to Gordon. He'd have killed you if I had."

The cook was grinning slightly. "She didn't protest to Gordon," he said, "but she waited until they camped and went to sleep. Then she crawled over to me and waked me. Afterwards she went out to the horse guard. She got his own gun away from him, held it against his side while I tied him up. Then we turned the rest of the horses loose so they couldn't follow and started back to pick you and Bill up."

Andy stared at them. "You put Gordon and the crew afoot? Where are they?"

"About ten miles down the trail."

"And you saw no Indians on the way back?"

"We'd hardly be here if we had."

"You've got no business to be here, anyhow," Andy told them. "You should have headed straight out for the fort."

"And left you and Bill alone, tied up?" It was the girl and a hint of temper had returned to her tone. "Andrew Drake! I don't know what I'm going to do with you. You're the hardest person in the world to get along with. Nothing anyone else ever does seems to satisfy you."

Andy used his good arm to pull her close. "Listen, Bantam, I'm not trying to quarrel with you."

"And don't call me Bantam."

He tightened his arm and kissed her. For a moment she held away from him, then the tension in her body relaxed. Her lips parted a little, and she whispered against them: "Oh, Andy, if you had only kissed me sooner, if you had just held me tight when I was so scared, maybe none of this would have happened."

The cook said in a disapproving tone: "You two better leave off loving and start worrying about your hair. There's a time and a place for everything."

Andy ignored him, holding the girl for a moment longer, caught by the rising surge of his own pent up feeling. "Bantam, honey. I'm sorry, I . . ."

But Mary Thorne broke the embrace. "Pop's right, Andy. There's a time and a place for everything."

He came back to reality slowly, a tired man, an exhausted man with a crippled arm, with a girl and a seventy-year-old gaffer on his hands. They were in the middle of a desert wilderness, with very little water and almost no food. He said calmly: "You came away without the gold? I must have been very important to you, Bantam. You came a long way to find that gold."

The cook's voice sharpened. "I wanted to take some with us, but she wouldn't let me go back after it. I tell you, she's been going crazy all day, thinking about you tied up back there. She'd probably have made the break sooner if I had let her. What's the matter, Andy, can't you under-stand how she feels about you?"

Andy passed a hand over his tired eyes. "I guess I'm not thinking very straight at the moment. I'm sorry, Bantam. I just can't quite believe it . . . even yet."

"I don't blame you." Her tone was low. "I guess we were meant to fight. I've said a lot of things that hurt you. It almost seemed that I delighted in hurting you. I . . ."

"If we don't get out of here," the cook insisted, "you will get hurt. You'll have more fighting than you bargain for, and you won't be fighting each other, either." He glanced at the eastern sky. "It's going to be light in an hour or two. What do we do now?"

Andy was silent, thinking of the long, weary miles that separated them from Fort Grant. His arm pained him and he felt his dizziness coming back. "We've two choices," he said. "One, we can rejoin the crew. With Indians about that would probably be the safer way. Where are they camped?"

"At Dobson's Wells."

"I wonder what they will do without horses."

"Try and walk into the fort probably. There are still ten men."

"Can they make it?"

The cook shrugged. "Depends on where your three missing Apaches are, and whether there were more in the band."

"There's your answer," Andy said, and looked at

the girl. "We either rejoin the crew or we try to cut through the hills and make the fort on our own."

"Gordon would kill you," she told him, "and he'd probably kill the cook for helping me escape. We'd better try the hills."

Studying her, Andy wondered if she realized exactly what this decision could mean. But her voice was steady; she had shown no hesitation. He started to protest, then changed his mind. It was a gamble any way you looked at it, but at least they had horses.

"We'll get back farther into the hills," he decided. "At daylight we'll find a place to hide and rest until tomorrow evening. We'll be short of water, but we may find some along the way."

XV

The spot they chose was well up on one of the lesser peaks that made a saw-tooth line that ran eastward only to split into a series of interlocking cañons that drained downward into the distant San Pedro. The camp provided a wide view of the twisted, jumbled land, a kind of look-out that covered the miles over which they had just come.

Despite protests, Andy insisted on taking the first watch while the cook and the girl slept. As the sun rose higher and higher in the almost cloudless sky, the very ground seemed to heave and shift under the glare. He knew this was only a trick of his tired eyes, that the heat shimmer was a normal thing, eddying in little swirls in the windless air. It required an effort to keep awake, an effort to rivet his attention on the barren landscape. And then he came sharply awake as the sound of guns echoed across the stillness.

They were a long way off, far in the west. He listened. He tried to pierce the distance, yet saw nothing. The sun was high, almost in the center of the sky, marking the time as accurately as any watch.

Behind him someone stirred. He turned to see the old cook rise and come forward to his side. Pop listened intently to the distant smatter of shots.

"Seems like your Indians caught up with Gordon and the crew," he said.

"Maybe," said Andy. "Or maybe it's a patrol out from Fort Grant or Fort Apache."

The cook shook his head. "Not steady enough. The Army controls its fire. I wonder what will happen to that gold. I was so close to it that I felt it with my hands. If the Apaches wipe out the crew . . ."

"They won't," said Andy. "That's a tough bunch. Bill trained them well." It was strange, thinking of Bill as a dead man, back up there among the rocks, with the Indians' bodies scattered around him. But as long as the crew lived and fought, a part of Bill Drake would live.

"Maybe," said the cook, "but if any of them get killed that were carrying the gold, it'll be there beside them. The Indians have very little use for the stuff."

"They're smart," Andy said. "A full water bottle and a bullet pouch means a lot more to them."

"Sure," said the cook. "Sure. Now you get some sleep. It's my turn to watch."

Andy moved back among the rocks, trying to find a little shade. The girl still slept, curled on her side like a small child, utterly exhausted. He stood for an instant, looking down at her, then found his own spot and stretched out.

He slept, although his dreams were troubled, and he came awake with a hand resting lightly on his shoulder. Mary Thorne knelt beside him and it was almost dark.

His head ached dully from the heat, but his arm did not seem to be paining and a cooler draft of air was coming down the small draw behind them to make life a little bearable. He sat up, looking around. Something was wrong with the camp, but he could not think what it was.

Pop! The cook should have been over there, watching the sweeping valley below. But maybe he had gone down to check the horses.

"Pop just move out?" he asked Mary.

She shook her head. "He rode out four hours ago to have a closer look at the fight."

Andy swore and came to his feet. "I should have known he'd try something like that. The gold was bothering him." He fell to cursing the gold under his breath. "What did he say to you?"

The girl was frightened. "He said he'd be back in a couple of hours." She turned and pointed to a ridge that showed faintly in the southwest through the advancing blue smokiness of the evening. "He thought he could see the fight from over there."

Andy began gathering up the water bottle and rifles. "Help me," he said. "We've got to move out."

She started. "Without Pop?"

"We can't help him," Andy said. "My guess is if he were coming back, he'd be here already. If he's run into trouble, they'll backtrack him. The sooner we get going, the better. . . . The old fool, why did he have to try this? Why does a man risk his life for gold?"

She said thoughtfully: "He told me he'd never come so close to that much gold in all his life."

Something in her voice made Andy look at her sharply. "Bantam," he said, "just how important was that gold to you? If Gordon and the men started to walk to the fort, they probably split the gold up between them with each man carrying something like twenty pounds. That's a lot to carry in this country, especially if you've got a rifle and food and water."

240

She frowned at him. "What are you trying to tell me, Andy?"

"That if the Apaches hit them, they probably got rid of the gold and it's scattered from hell to breakfast right now. We can swing down and take a look, if you want, but we may lose our hair doing it."

She was silent, considering. "The gold means a lot," she said in a small voice. "It means saving our ranch, and taking care of my father."

He put his good arm around her, drawing her close. "We aren't going to get it, Bantam. You know that."

He kissed her then, tenderly, feeling his own passion rise. "I love you." The words were not much more than a whisper. "I don't know when I started loving you. Maybe the first time I saw you on the trail, maybe when I saw how scared you were at the blood on Wakeman's saddle. I guess that's why I've acted as I have. I'm not used to women, Bantam. I don't understand them. I'm not very good at trying to explain, either."

"You're doing all right." Her arms tightened convulsively about him. "I was afraid I'd lost you. I'm still afraid."

"Don't be," he told her. "Fear doesn't do any good. It doesn't help at all."

"Yesterday I didn't want to die," she told him. "I guess no one ever really wants to die, but today I feel more than that. I don't just want to stay alive.

I want to *live*. I feel as if I've never really lived yet, but with you I can. With you I can find out what life really means." She pressed closer as if trying to enfold him with her body.

He held her closely, saying quietly: "We'll live, Bantam. I know we will. We'll go eastward, across the hills. We can't wait for the cook. It would do him no good if we did, but somehow we'll get through. All the Apaches in Arizona won't stop us now."

He kissed her again before he let her go, then picked up the rifle and led her down toward the horses.

At the box cañon she had to help him onto the Indian pony because of his useless arm, but, after they mounted, he grinned at her and led the way eastward. They traveled by the stars, trying to put as much between them and the valley as possible.

At dawn they made a waterless camp, high up in the rocks.

Andy watched while Mary slept, and, after the sun had reached its peak, he waked her and settled down for his own rest. But tired as he was, sleep did not come easily. His arm ached and he felt his armpit where a telltale lump might herald blood poisoning. There was no lump. His body relaxed, but his mind sharpened. *I've got to get her safely out of this.*

He dozed then, and the next he knew Mary was bending over him, her hand pressed tightly against his mouth. He opened his eyes and saw the fear in her face.

His lips moved against her palm. "What is it?"

"Indians." It was a whisper. "Three of them . . . down by the horses."

He nodded and rolled over, coming carefully to his knees. He crawled across the tiny sandy bowl to the sheltering rocks, searching the slope below.

He had tethered the horses in a small side ravine where there was little dry grass, but had chosen to camp 200 feet above. For a time he saw no movement at all. Then he caught a sudden shifting at the mouth of the ravine and for an instant had a clear view of an Apache as the Indian examined the slope above him. Soon the man faded behind a rock.

Andy held the six-gun that the girl had brought with her from Gordon's camp and had all the Indians been in sight he might have tried to get them. But he did not know where the others were and he did not want to disclose his location. He squatted there, hesitating. Had it been dark he would have tried to retreat over the rim behind them, hoping to stay in country so rough that the savages could only follow them on foot. But the sun was still a good two hours from dusk in the cloudless sky.

He thrust the girl's six-gun into his belt and picked up her rifle. It was one of the new Winchesters. Had it been the Apache gun he had taken, an old cap-and-ball affair, he would not have been certain of his mark, but now he thrust the newer rifle over one of the stones, using it as a rest since he could only move one arm. He waited.

Time stretched out. Nothing stirred below him. He thought the Apaches might have picked up his sign on the hillside below, guessed his hiding place, and be circling.

Suddenly a mounted Indian appeared in the mouth of the ravine. Almost instantly Andy's rifle sent out its sharp, whip-like report, echoing down through the rocks until it was multiplied twenty times. He saw the rider's hands go high, saw him plunge headlong from the bare back of the horse—and suddenly Andy was under fire from two directions.

Apparently he had been right. The two remaining savages had been circling, creeping up on his hiding place from two directions, and the rider must have been a decoy to draw him into the open. They must have believed that the danger of losing his horses would force him to show himself. But Andy did not shift from his rock shelter. He was not too worried by their fire since it was obvious by the spacing of their shots that there were only two, and that their guns were cap-and-ball models that needed reloading after each discharge. He did regret the horses, since he had no idea whether he would ever be able to recapture them, but what worried him most was fear that the sound of firing would bring other Indians. With the Winchester and the six-gun he was far better armed, but if he had a dozen savages to contend with, he would have no hope. His only chance was that the rest of the band was still occupied with Gordon and the crew.

But all this was useless speculation, so he put it from his mind. He had not answered their fire since he could see nothing on the rocky slope to shoot at, and their shots were coming at more infrequent intervals. Perhaps, he thought, they were low on ammunition. If they had been raiding in the hills for long this might well be the case. For that matter he had no shells to spare himself.

He waited, watching carefully, taking a moment's glance now and then to measure the distance between sun and horizon. In his strained imagination it seemed that the sun failed to move at all. But finally the red disc dipped toward the mountains to the west, and the purple shadows lengthened, spreading to fill the hollows, dulling the sharp outlines of the rough terrain.

The girl was crouched behind him, low and motionless. She held the Indian rifle he had stolen, as if the one charge it contained were a last reserve.

Andy took time to reload the Winchester and his belt gun, never lifting his eyes from the slope.

"We've got to be ready," he warned. "As soon as it's dark enough, they'll rush us."

"What do we do?" The girl's voice was small but perfectly steady and he had a momentary feeling of high pride in her courage. Whatever Mary Thorne's faults, she bore up under pressure. Fear didn't drive her into panic. It made her fight back.

"We wait," he said. "We wait until dark, little Bantam, and then we move ourselves."

XVI

They crept out just before deep dark, working their way up the rim, slipping around boulders like two shadows.

Andy went first, the six-gun in his good hand. The girl followed, carrying the Winchester because she had two good arms to use it. The Indian rifle had been discarded as almost useless.

Luck favored them in that the moon did not rise until after ten, and, by the time they gained the rim, it was so dark that the girl kept a hand on Andy's shoulder to guide herself.

Just under the rim Andy veered right. The sky still had a trace of reflected light and he did not want them to show against its backdrop lest the sharp eyes of their attackers spot the haze of movement. And he had no intention of traveling the rough country ahead with the red wolves clinging to his trail. He knew that the Indians' stamina was far greater than theirs, that they could not shake the Apaches off, that sooner or later the savages would close in and finish them.

The time for a showdown had come, and he waited only for the proper place before he turned to fight. He found it finally, a break in the rimrock where they could slip through a cleft without climbing over the crest. Here he paused and turned back, placing his lips tightly against the girl's ear so that she heard through the movement of his lips rather than through any sound he made.

"Go on. Wait beyond the top. If I don't call to you after the fight, move out. Keep headed east until you strike the military road, keep your gun ready and the last bullet for yourself." She faltered for an instant. "Don't argue," he said, and kissed her fully on the mouth, stopping her protest. Then he was gone, slipping back in the dark, returning carefully the way they had come.

He smelled the Indians before he saw them—the rancid odor from their greasy hair that he had learned long before to recognize. They came through the rocks, shadows so dark that they blended perfectly into the background. They came almost noiselessly, feeling their way. He never knew how he came to see them, for it was so dark that he could hardly see the ground itself. He squatted, waiting, at one side of a huge boulder, holding his fire until he would have some chance of getting them both. But they turned, cutting to the left around the stone, and he lost them in the night. He cursed silently in the darkness. He should have fired when he first glimpsed them. It had been a mistake to wait, a mistake that might well cost both his and the girl's life.

He rose, not daring to stay where he was since they might well work past him in the darkness and find the girl below the rim. He moved upward around the rock that was almost as large as a house. Climbing, he abruptly found himself face to face with one of the braves. Not five feet separated them as the first savage crawled over the rock shoulder. The second warrior followed directly behind the leader, but too close to bring up his rifle properly. They were as startled as Andy. For an instant three enemies froze as if all had become a part of the stone on which they crouched.

It was the leading Indian who recovered first. He had been carrying the rifle in the crook of his arm while he used his other hand to help his progress. Still on his knees, he swung the gun muzzle around to bear on Andy.

Andy saw the motion. He forced his maimed arm to knock the rifle barrel aside while he brought up his six-gun with his good hand. The guns exploded together, their reports blending into a single sound. The muzzle blast from the Indian's gun burned along the side of Andy's face, but the heavy bullet whistled harmlessly past his ear. His own gun had spoken almost against the savage's bare chest. The heavy slug seemed to lift the man and hurl him into the arms of his companion. The second Indian tried to roll out of the way, but only lost his balance and fell backward, sliding down the rough face of the rock.

Andy went after him, scrambling crab-fashion, until he too lost his balance and rolled down the rough face. He heard the Indian shout, an unintelligible cry that could have been fear or defiance. He did not know which. He had no chance to determine exactly what had happened.

They fell together into a wedge-shaped patch of ground between the rocks. The Indian was partly on top. He had lost his rifle, but he had his knife. He raised himself, confident now that he had the white man at his mercy. Andy shot him three times, pulling the revolver's trigger as fast as he could re-cock it. The Indian slumped, his knife falling into the ground beside Andy's ear, his sweaty rancid body stretched across Andy's chest, pinning him to the ground. Andy lay there, too shocked by the sudden ending of the action to move, for a full minute. Then he roused himself and managed to work his way from under the dead man.

It was harder to climb out of the trap between the rocks, hindered as he was by his nearly useless arm. He called to the girl from the top of the rock and heard her cry of joy as she answered. Then he turned to stare at the dark valley below. Somewhere down there were his horses, and perhaps some that the Indians had ridden. He had no way of knowing where they were hidden, and there might well be other Indians.

It was a choice he had to make, and he made it more willingly with the knowledge that the country through which they would be forced to travel was so rough that a horse might prove to be a liability. He turned back then and climbed to the rim, calling softly—"Bantam, Bantam."—until he located her and felt her slight body trembling against him in the darkness. "It's all right," he whispered. "They're dead."

She shivered, standing against him, her hands on his shoulders. "Andy, oh, Andy darling." It was as if in his name she had discovered a new word, in the night she had discovered a new life. She raised her mouth for his kiss and they stood thus for a long time. Finally he pushed her gently away.

"There might be other Indians below. We'd better get moving while we can."

"The horses?"

He shrugged. "Lord knows where ours are. That first Apache I killed was riding them off. As for the Indian mounts, they might be anywhere. We could spend two days looking for them and we might run into other Indians. Are you game to try and walk out? The country we'll have to travel wasn't made for horses, Bantam. We might have to abandon them anyhow."

She asked in a small voice: "Can we make it?"

He wanted to reassure her, but he knew that no lie he could tell would be convincing. "God knows . . . the best we can do is try. We've got enough dried meat for three or four days. If we have to, there's mesquite and prickly pear." He tried to laugh and did not make too good a job of it. "At least, without horses we'll only need to hunt water for ourselves."

"Will we find enough?"

He did not know. The only other way would be to return to the valley through which Gordon had led the crew, and thus stand a far greater chance of running into the main body of the Indians. Of the two choices he preferred the mountains. If he had to die, he would choose thirst over the savage torture of the Apaches.

He thrust the six-gun under his belt and took the Winchester from Mary. They had no blanket now to carry, nothing but the half-filled water bottle and the small packet of dried meat.

Thus they started over the rim, moving ever eastward, searching for the military road from Fort Apache that ran down off the Mogollon plateau through the San Carlos to Fort Grant, on the San Pedro.

Neither of them expected to make it. Both were certain that they would die among the dry peaks. But neither wanted the other to guess the stark fear that gripped the secret heart.

XVII

They camped an hour after daybreak, having put nearly ten miles between them and the ridge where Andy had killed the Indians. It was higher here, and cooler, and they found a seep that netted them enough water for a morning drink. Afterward they curled up in the shadow of some rocks, both too exhausted to care how far they had traveled or how many Indians followed them.

Andy fought to keep awake, to watch the trail over which they had just labored. He saw nothing but the barren emptiness shimmering in the morning sun, and finally he slept.

He awoke in the late afternoon and aroused Mary. The cut in his forearm was red and angry-looking, but the swelling had gone down and he found that he could use the arm to a certain extent. Encouraged, he scooped out a little hole below the tiny spring, watched it fill slowly with water, and gave Mary a drink.

After his own drink, he filled the bottle, and then they bathed the arm, their faces, and finally their swollen feet. The girl's boots were cracked and Andy eyed them with alarm. Boots were more important than guns in this country.

Just before full dark they threaded their way from a small ravine, then up a narrow cañon, climbing a rock wall, breasting the shoulder of the mountain, and coming slowly down on the other side.

There seemed no end to the everlasting peaks, to the rise and fall of the hard-baked earth. That night they found no water, and all the next day they nursed what little remained in the bottle. At nightfall on the second day they started out, thin and worn, each with a small pebble under the tongue in an effort to keep some saliva flowing, but they had not covered more than a mile before the girl stumbled and went down.

Andy dropped the rifle, stooped, and picked her up, feeling her quivering under his hands. "Easy, Bantam," he crooned. "We'll rest a little while and go on."

She sat on a small boulder, crying softly. "I'm sorry," she said. "I'm so tired. I can't go on. I can't. I can't. I can't."

He shook her then, realizing that she was on the verge of hysteria. When at last she relaxed against him, he steadied her with his good arm about her thin shoulders. "It's all right. Just rest. You'll be all right with a little rest."

"You go," she told him when she could steady

her voice. "Alone you might stand some chance of coming through."

"No," he said. "Rest."

"It's my fault, I . . ."

He held her tightly with the good arm. "Rest, Bantam."

She went to sleep finally against his shoulder, so soundly asleep that she did not even wake when he eased her to the ground. He knelt for a moment, looking down at her, knowing that they were through, that this was the finish, that the kindest thing he could do was to put the barrel of the six-gun against her temple and squeeze the trigger. In that way she would escape the needless suffering that would go on and on until they fell, blind and crazed for lack of water, too weak then to use the gun that might bring them relief.

He drew the gun and bent forward. The moonlight fell directly on her face, and, just as he placed the end of the barrel against her head, she stirred and smiled in her sleep. One small hand fluttered against his rough fingers, guided there by a dream. As the hand touched, it closed tightly and held.

He choked and dropped the gun as if the walnut stock had suddenly turned red hot in his grasp. He sank down beside her and sobbed dry, rasping sobs that tore at his throat and shook his body until he, too, slept.

• • •

The next morning they found the burned-out ranch. It had never been much of a ranch, just a building, part stone, and therefore only part burned, a pole corral that the Indians had not even bothered to destroy, and a spring. The place had been abandoned for a long time. The ashes were bleached and scattered, and the spring was so sand-choked that hardly a trickle ran out. But it trickled and they both fell beside it, burying their faces against the damp earth. Afterward he cleaned it out, enlarging to the rock walls that the forgotten rancher had built so carefully so long ago.

They drank, and, when the rock basin had partly filled, they bathed their faces, and then, stripping off their boots, soaked their feet. Sitting there, her small feet in the clear water, her hair damp around her forehead, Mary looked at Andy and laughed.

"This," she said, "should teach me. Only last night I was ready to give up."

Andy didn't answer. He had a clear memory of a gun in his hand, pressed against her temple. He shuddered.

"What's the matter?" she asked anxiously. "Your arm?"

"Arm's all right." He managed to speak steadily. "I was just thinking of a mistake I nearly made."

"A mistake?"

"Forget it." His tone was almost rough. "It isn't

important." He rose and started to strip off his shirt, but had so much trouble that Mary came to help him. She insisted on washing the arm and re-bandaging it. Then she turned and looked at the rocked-in spring.

"You know, that's almost big enough for me to sit in." Andy said—"Huh?"—but she paid no attention to him. Instead she began unfastening her torn shirt. A moment later the dust-caked pants fell away. She stood, slim and white, in the hot glare of the morning sun.

Andy's first reaction was one of sheer amazement; his next, that she was the most beautiful thing he had ever seen. She stood there without a hint of self-consciousness for a moment, stretching her arms to loft the stiff muscles of her young body, her breasts standing out round and erect and firm. Then she stepped into the cool water, shivering a little from the sheer joy of its coolness, and settled herself into the natural bathtub that the rock walls made.

"Darling, it's wonderful." She ducked her head, washing the dust from her hair. "I've never been so dirty in my whole life. Get some sand and rub it across my back. I feel like I'll never be clean again."

He rubbed her back, trembling a little as his hands touched the soft skin. He had never felt quite this way before. He wondered if it was because he was so tired. He had known other women. No one who had lived in frontier towns could fail to know them. But not one of them had ever aroused him as this girl did. He could not understand how she could sit there unconcernedly in the little pool, feeling his hands upon her.

"Bantam."

She turned to peek up at him.

"Oh, Bantam." He dropped to his knees on the moist earth and his arms went around her, drawing her close to him. "Bantam, darling."

She smiled then, and her hands went up to his hair. She pulled his mouth against hers, holding it there for one long memorable moment. Then she pushed him away. "You haven't had your bath yet," she said.

He gaped at her, saw that she was laughing at him, and suddenly he reached down and lifted her out of the spring. She gave a little shriek, struggling in his grasp. It was hard to hold her with one arm.

"Andy, let me down."

"No."

"Let me down, please. I haven't any clothes on." She said this as if she had made a sudden, distressing discovery. "Andy, this isn't right."

"What isn't?"

She did not know quite whether to laugh or be angry. "A pretty picture we make."

"Don't we."

"What if someone should see us?" For a moment

she stared around. Then reality came back. She said—"I'm a fool, aren't I?"—and kissed him.

"You're a pretty one," he told her, and put her down. Somehow a certain restraint had grown up between them in that last minute that had not been there before.

The girl turned away. She made no effort to dress, but she did manage to keep her back toward him as she rinsed her clothes. Next she picked up his shirt and washed it. "You know," she picked up the theme again, "you'd feel better after a bath."

He hesitated. Like most males he was inclined to an inherent modesty without truly thinking about it. The girl noticed his hesitation and walked to a seat beside the old stone wall of the burned cabin, close to where she had hung her clothes to dry.

He watched her for a moment, small and white, then called: "You'd better put something over your shoulders! This sun will blister you!" Getting no answer, he peeled off his pants and settled himself in the spring. The water was incredibly cool and caressing as it settled around his tired body. It seemed to engulf his cares, his worries. He lay back, head against one of the rocks, and felt the moisture seep into him. It was as if the pores of his dry skin had opened like so many tiny mouths and were drinking their fill. Afterward he climbed out and washed his stained pants, then his socks. His shirt, which the girl had spread on the ground, was almost dry from the intense heat of the noon sun. He donned it and, still feeling half naked, carried the pants across the yard to spread them over a boulder.

When he came back, he found that the girl had dressed and was curled up in the shade of the wall. He joined her and fell asleep within five minutes. How long he slept he was not certain, but a sound brought him up on his good elbow, alert and motionless. For a moment he had no idea what had caused the sound that had awakened him. Then he saw a deer, hardly half grown, stealing out of the brush toward the spring. He lay there, watching it. The animal was careful, but, because the humans were downwind, it had not caught their scent. Andy lay there, glancing over toward the girl. She still slept and his great fear was that she might stir and scare the deer away. The Winchester rested only two feet from his hand, leaning against the broken wall where, with the frontier instinct, he had placed it, ever close.

He straightened, almost holding his breath. The deer was less than 200 feet away now, almost at the spring. It came on daintily, yet suspiciously, pausing now and then to raise its slender nose and sniff the air.

Andy had the rifle in his good hand. Given full use of his other arm, he could have made a casual, easy shot. But now, even with the greatest care, he could miss. This small animal just lowering its head for the first drink meant so very, very much to them if he hit it. He did not even dare let himself consider the full meaning of a miss. He pushed the barrel of the gun out for support on his hunched knees and sighted along the barrel. He drew a bead directly behind the left shoulder, just as the deer raised its head for a quick look. This whip-like report echoed and reëchoed through the rocks of the barren hillsides. The girl jerked awake, jumping quickly to her feet, quick terror mirrored on her startled face.

"Andy, what is it?"

He was already on his feet, pointing the still smoking gun at the silent body beside the spring.

"Food," he said, "real, honest food." Then he sprinted to where the deer lay. Saliva filled his mouth as he set to work. He skinned the deer with frantic haste, but built the fire carefully, so there would be no smoke. The smell of burning would be caught quickly by any Indian. He was taking a chance with any fire, and he knew it. But danger couldn't quell hunger. After all, if the rifle shot hadn't brought Indians down upon them, the fire seemed a small chance to take. Besides, a chance to eat fresh-cooked meat was more than any famished man could resist.

They ate slowly, with utter, silent relish, roasting the meat upon pointed sticks before the fire. They gorged themselves, and, after they had rested, groaning at the fullness of their bellies, Andy cut strips for drying, spreading them carefully upon the flat stones.

Finally they slept, not beside the spring, but high up in the rocks above so that, if any intruders came to the spring, they would not be caught unaware.

The second day at the burned ranch was much easier. They breakfasted heavily on the deer, and then rested through the morning, husbanding their strength.

After the noon meal they stretched out in the shade of the stone wall, the girl's head against Andy's shoulder, staring out across the wasteland they had crossed.

"Will we make it?"

Her eyes were closed when he glanced down at her face. She was thin, but some of the marks of suffering had already been erased by water and food.

"Of course," he said, and wondered at the ease with which the words came. It was hard to recapture the anguish of the last two days before they had reached the ranch. It seemed as if they had been part of a nightmare that was unbelievable, unrelated to himself. Yet the country they still must travel was as rugged as any they had seen. They were still far from the military road, much farther from the fort.

"You know," she said, "I almost hate to leave

here. It's been so restful, so utterly quiet. I've never really been alone with you before."

His eyes swept the vacant land. "We're certainly alone now, Bantam."

"And you haven't kissed me. Not once since yesterday."

Suddenly the easy companionship that they had shared was gone, replaced by an awareness such as he had experienced at the spring. His arm tightened convulsively and he bent to kiss her. He felt the warm response of her lips under his, felt them part a little, and knew that the tip of her small tongue caressed him.

He pulled himself away with a physical effort. "Easy, Bantam, easy. We'd better wait for the rest of it until we get back to civilization."

"Why, Andy?"

He laughed, a shaky sound that held no mirth even in his own ears. "You should know better than I. Aren't women supposed to have a sort of instinct for self-protection?"

She said softly: "You don't know a great deal about women, do you? You're like Bill in some ways, but you're much nicer than he was."

Andy did not want to talk about Bill and said so.

She shook her head. "I've got to," she told him. "I've got to get it off my chest, the way I feel about him, because it's all tied up with the way I feel about you. Bill was hard and I was afraid of him. He killed, and I was more afraid. I hated him because he seemed utterly ruthless. But I realize now that his hardness was a shell, that deep down underneath he had a lot of kindness, a lot of feeling for others, yet he was afraid of it, afraid that his kindness might betray him."

Andy looked at her wonderingly. "What has all this got to do with me?"

She smiled and, reaching up, twisted a lock of his hair around her finger. "Because you have that same kindness. You don't fight it as Bill did, but you still try to conceal it, even from yourself. You're being kind now. You're protecting me from yourself where another man would already have had his way with me."

Andy's breath caught in his throat. "Stop it," he said hoarsely. "I'm only human."

"Yes," she told him softly. "And I'm human, too, Andy. Men always think women don't have the same desires that they do, because the woman is the one who's supposed to hang back. I love you, you fool. I want you. We may never get out of these hills. We may never have a life like ordinary people, but I want to know you at least once. Please, Andy, please . . ."

She raised her lips for his kiss. Then she drew away. He felt her fingers fumbling between them as she unbuttoned her shirt. Then she took his hand and pressed it against her bared breast.

"Please, Andy."

He took her then. It was like nothing he had ever dreamed of, never dared to imagine. Her body was alive, demanding, yet yielding, a miracle of sinuous, sensuous motion.

"Darling . . ." They were lying under the warmth of the afternoon sun, feeling its strengthening rays on their bare flesh. "Darling . . ."

He kissed her again. It seemed impossible that there could be any desire left in them, but there was. Again they shared the joy that only they could give to each other, and then they slept.

It was dark when they awakened. They ate, silent, having no need for words, and then they packed the fried meat and had their last drink at the spring. They filled the water bottle and turned eastward, reluctant to leave the only place where either had known full happiness.

Three days later they struggled down off the bench, footsore and weary, their water almost exhausted, and came out into the clear-cut wheel tracks of the military road.

XVIII

Lieutenant Frank B. Carter, escorting the paymaster's wagon with his detail of ten troopers, rounded the long sweeping curve of the trail and checked his horse. A day out of Fort Apache, heading southward toward Grant, he had certainly not expected to see a woman step from the brush before him.

Carter had only served for eleven months in the territory, but at the moment he suspected that he was a victim of the desert madness that the old-timers were supposed to develop after years in these barren hills.

The troopers behind him, lank and burned out from much riding, pulled to a halt behind Carter, their thin sunburned faces showing an amazement as great as that of their officer.

The girl had stepped to the center of the trail, facing them. A moment later she was joined by a ragged scarecrow of a man who carried his left arm in a makeshift sling.

Carter, after his first jolt of surprise, walked his horse forward and dismounted. The men pressed up until they made a circle around Andy and the girl. They listened to the story with evident disbelief.

Afterward Carter ordered them into the pay-master's ambulance, and the detail started south at the double.

Mary Thorne sat on the wagon's hard seat, dipping sparingly from the canteen that Carter had pressed upon her gallantly, and stared outward through the raised flats as they swirled along the bottom of a narrow cañon, cutting across a side ravine, dropping ever downward into the heat and dust of the valley of the San Pedro. Along this they ran, Mary deriving a sense of comfort and security from the *creak* of the troopers saddles, the grind of the wagon, and the shouts of its driver. It was very good to be among people again, to know that there were ten guns between her and any chance Apaches. She laced the fingers of her left hand into those of Andy and sighed deeply as she looked at his pain-lined face.

"It's over," she said softly. "We made it. We're safe, and I never thought we would be safe again."

Andy had not thought so, either. The rest at the old ranch and the deer meat had given them the strength to push on, but the way had seemed endless as mile after weary mile of rough country unfolded before them without any sign of the wheel tracks of the military road.

Entirely out of water, they had struggled grimly, hoping that each new cañon would show some signs of moisture that might lead them upward to an unknown seep. Finally they had settled down on a rocky ridge, too beaten to struggle, ready to admit that there was no hope. And then somewhere out of the northeast they had heard the sound of horses—shod horses. Next came the *jingle* of ambulance harness and the grind of its wheels.

It had seemed absurd that they could have been so close to the trail without realizing it and that they might have stayed in the rocks until they dried up and died without ever guessing that the wheel tracks of the road lay only a quarter of a mile away.

Andy dozed. His arm, which had seemed to be healing properly at the ranch, was now swollen and angry-looking. He was light-headed from exhaustion and a slight fever, and by the time they came to the junction where the dry wash of Aravaipa Creek cut down to join the main cañon, he was too near delirium to realize that they had reached their journey's end.

The ambulance dipped across the wash, climbed the far side to the square made by the adobe buildings that were Fort Grant, and pulled into the parade ground.

Andy Drake was helped from the hard seat by two of the troopers, but he shook off their hands and managed to straighten up and look around. Men were spilling out of quarters to greet the detail, and below the fort he saw the tents and brush wickiups of the friendly Indian camp. With Carter conducting them, they walked across the parade to the long adobe. Officers appeared on the brush porch and Carter reported.

"Paymaster's detail from Fort Apache, sir, with two civilians, one a woman."

Then Andy saw Mary Thorne step forward and heard Major Howdy's rumble of surprise at her appearance.

"Good Lord, ma'am. Good Lord. You look as if you've had a very trying time, very."

And heard Mary's answer as she said: "We have had . . . a very trying time, Major."

And afterward, he could not be certain exactly how long, Andy was pacing beside an orderly as the soldier led him away toward the doctor. They crossed a corner of the baked parade ground and came up to the *ramada* of the medical officer's adobe. There remained enough evening light to see, although the sun was well down enough for Andy to recognize the big figure that stepped out from the porch at their approach.

"Monte!"

Monte Gordon stopped. He had paid no attention to the two men crossing toward him. He stood for an instant, utterly motionless. Then he said in a voice that sounded curiously flat: "You . . . you're alive?"

"I'm alive," Andy said, and strangely the fogginess that had clouded his brain for days faded away. "I'm alive, but Bill is dead."

"Is he?" said Gordon. He had recovered completely. He even seemed pleased. "I suppose you know that the cook and the girl left us. They're probably dead, too."

"The cook may be," Andy told him, "but the girl isn't. She's over there now, talking to the commander. You'll have some slight explaining to do, Monte."

Gordon's face darkened. "To hell with that. I've already told my story, including Bill's murder of

Wakeman." Positive joy gleamed in his eyes. "And for good measure I threw in your name. I believe in covering everything I can. I said I didn't know which of you actually killed Wakeman, but you were both there and both to blame. I told them where to find his body. I said I'd go into the territorial court and repeat the story when necessary. Does that cover it?"

"No," Andy said, "because I'm going to kill you."

Gordon looked at the useless arm in its ragged sling, at the drawn pain lines on the thin bearded face, and he laughed. "Boy," he said, "you got yourself mixed up. You're not Bill Drake. You're Andy. You're the kid that started riding with us only a few months ago, so don't tempt me. I'd like nothing better than to kill you and not hang for it, but the Army has funny ways. They wouldn't take kindly to a gunfight on their precious parade ground."

"Never mind," Andy said. "I'd rather kill you either way. It's your choice. Go for it."

His own right hand moved toward the holstered gun as he spoke. He had no real idea of how fast Gordon was and at the moment he did not care. For days he had held himself together, had driven himself with the idea that somewhere, somehow he would find this man Gordon if he still lived.

He saw Gordon's lips twist as if in hunger, a wolfish grin. He knew that the man wanted to kill him. There was a lot between them, all the friction of the trip, all the burning resentment that he felt for the man who had left them to die. And then there was the girl.

Later, the orderly who was accompanying Andy described the fight to an interested audience in the big barracks.

"Gordon's hand went down," the man said, "and then it seemed to come up like a magic trick, all full of the gun. I didn't see Drake draw. I was too busy diving out of the way. I heard two shots as I hit the ground, then I twisted and saw Drake. He was on his feet, even though he'd been hit in the side. I saw him sway. I saw him bring his gun up slowly. It came up so slow that Gordon shot again. But he was shooting too fast. If he'd taken his time, he couldn't have missed. He got panicky, I guess . . . but, hell, who wouldn't have lost his nerve when he'd put two bullets into a man and he didn't fall down. Anyhow, Drake finally got his gun up. It couldn't have taken more than a second, of course, but it seemed to me like it took an hour. He got it up, see, and he fired just once, real slow and deliberate. And so help me, he hit Gordon right over the heart."

That, also, although more elegantly, was the way the doctor told it to Mary Thorne. The doctor had been inside his office, and he did not have as good a view as did the orderly.

"I heard them talking," he said, "and I stepped to the door just as the gun play began. Gordon performed as fast a draw as I've ever seen. On the other hand, Drake moved like an old man, or as if his brain couldn't direct his hand properly. After I examined him, I wasn't surprised. The man was sick, threatened with blood poison, reduced to skin and bones. He was wounded before he even squeezed the trigger. He fired only once, and Gordon went down. Drake stood over him, looking down at the dead man. Then he holstered his gun and said . . . 'It's all finished, Bill. I paid him off for leaving you. I took care of him.'" The doctor shook his head. "I helped the orderly carry Drake in. I didn't think he would live, and I still don't quite understand. . . ."

Andy had no real memory of the fight. He said that from the time Gordon's hand moved down toward his gun, his memory stopped. He regained consciousness three days later, but he didn't know where he was until he recognized Mary Thorne, sitting quietly beside his rope bed.

Mary told him other things. She said Monte Gordon was dead. She told him that Gordon and three other men from the crew had finally managed to fight their way through to the fort. Apparently they had run into Victorio's main band, and Victorio had become so engrossed in harrying Gordon that he made no effort to find out what happened to the seven braves who stayed behind to examine the deserted camp.

She told Andy that much, and then, on the doctor's orders, she left him alone. He lay for days in the close, hot room, looking out across the sun-drenched parade ground. He gained weight slowly, the cut in his arm healing long before the bullet holes. He saw no one but the doctor, the orderly, and Mary.

He knew nothing about the argument Mary Thorne had with the fort's commander. He knew nothing about the detail that rode out, back-tracking the route covered by Gordon and his men. He did not know that they had found the cook's body, scalped and violated, not over three miles from where the old man had left them.

And suddenly Andy was well enough to stand on his feet, to be helped to a chair, to sit on the adobe's porch and look out across the parade ground toward the rim of the distant White Mountains.

It was on the second morning after he had been allowed to get up that Mary Thorne came in to see him. He knew at once by her manner that something bothered her, but she did not speak until she had settled herself in the other chair.

"You're in bad trouble, Andy Drake," she told him. "Why in heaven's name did you have to shoot Monte Gordon?"

Andy was dumbfounded. He stared at her for a moment, unable to form the proper words, then defensive anger rose and almost choked him.

"Shoot Gordon? What else did you expect me to do? Didn't he leave Bill and me to die? In God's name, Bantam, I had to brace him. If I hadn't, he'd have run me clear out of the territory."

"Do you want to stay here? Why should you want to stay in this terrible land? Oh, Andy, it would have been so much better, so much easier. We could have gone to my ranch and . . ."

"Do you honestly believe he would have left you alone there? Don't forget, you'd made a deal with him. He was the kind of man who would have forced you to carry it out."

She colored angrily, but she managed to keep her voice level. "And if you had to shoot him, did you have to do it on an Army post? The major is furious. You'd be in the guard house this minute if it weren't for the doctor and me."

Andy glowered at her. "To the devil with the major."

"You can't say that!" she snapped. "The major is the authority here, and Gordon talked to him about you. He believes you killed Monte to keep him from testifying against you about Wakeman's murder."

"You know I had no part in killing Wakeman."

"That's what I told him. I even lied a little. I swore you were with me the whole time. But he won't believe me."

"Why?"

Her color rose. "Because he thinks that I'm not

an unprejudiced witness. He guessed that I love you."

"Let me talk to this major. . . ."

She laid a quick hand on his arm. "Listen to me, Andy. You don't seem to understand. You'll talk to him because you have to. Can't you see, you're practically under arrest. He's made up his mind to send you to Tucson under guard. He intends to turn you over to the United States marshal. You'll be held for trial in Wakeman's death."

Andy bit his lip. He had been in the territory long enough to know that Bill Drake and all his crew members were so thoroughly hated by both soldiers and civilians that none of them could possibly expect a fair hearing in any territorial court.

"Don't worry," he said finally. "I'll watch my tongue when I talk to the major."

But when the time came for him to talk with the post commander, he had trouble remembering his promise. The contrast between the two men was as extreme as could be found along the far-flung border.

The major had worn the uniform for over twenty years. He might continue to wear it for nearly twenty more, winding up his career with a general's stars and the reputation of being one of the nation's most brilliant Indian fighters. He had the prejudices of his class, a deep-rooted suspicion of most civilians, and a strong feeling that most of the trouble that forced him to battle the Indians was caused by such wild and unruly men as Bill and Andy Drake.

He came striding across the parade with the adjutant at his side. He stopped before Andy who was seated on the porch. Andy could have risen; his strength had returned surprisingly during his two days out of bed. But he had chosen to remain seated, feeling that he thus had the officer at a disadvantage.

The major felt this, also. He stared hard at this man who, in his own mind, he already had tried and convicted of murder. He was amazed at Andy's obvious youth, but he quickly reminded himself that some of the most dangerous outlaws the border had produced were hardly out of their teens.

He said a little pompously: "I'm Major Howdy. I haven't had a chance to question you since Gordon's death. The doctor insisted that you were not in condition to stand an inquiry." His tone showed plainly that he was not certain he agreed with the doctor.

Andy did not answer, and the major's tanned face deepened into red. When he next spoke, his tone gained the slightly rasping note that the men of the 3rd Cavalry knew so well.

"You chose to shoot a man on my parade ground," he said.

"He asked for it." Andy kept his voice so low

that the major had difficulty in hearing. "He'd have gotten it sooner, but I figured I needed him alive to fight the Indians."

The major was still angry, but he contained himself enough to say levelly: "I have no doubt that Monte Gordon left a lot to be desired as a citizen, but that still gives you no license to shoot him, especially on a military reservation."

That, Andy realized, was what bothered the major most—the shooting had taken place on the Fort Grant parade ground.

He did not know, of course, that the story of the gunfight would be told and retold, growing each time that it was repeated to impress a fresh batch of green recruits until the name of Andy Drake would become one of the bloody legends of the early days of the territory, and that his killing of Gordon would go down in history as one of the greatest duels of the ages. He only knew that, at the moment, he stood in direct danger, and that the man before him held his future in the palm of his hand.

The major knew this, too. He stood there, trying to control his anger, trying to be fair, yet knowing that, if this quiet man who sat motionlessly in the doctor's split-backed chair were subject to military law, he would have him court-martialed at once.

"You may not know," he said speaking carefully, "that Gordon made a statement about you. I can't well charge you with his murder, because both the orderly and the doctor agree that he drew first. In effect, then, you fired in self-defense. But Gordon swore that you and your brother murdered a lawyer outside of Tucson, a man named Wakeman. I intend to turn you over to the marshal for that murder."

"Gordon is dead," Andy said.

"Unfortunately for you his death does not close the matter. Before he died, he signed a statement, describing exactly how Wakeman's murder occurred. I think you're going to find that Mister Wakeman had a number of friends who will do everything in their power to see that you're brought to trial. As soon as the doctor will admit that you're well enough to travel, I'll send you in with an escort."

He turned then, executing as perfect an about-face as he had ever clicked off during his years at the Academy. He stalked back across the parade, straight and tall and representing the full majesty of the United States Army.

Andy watched him go, and his thoughts were bitter. It seemed a crowning irony that he should have escaped from the Apaches only to be tried for his life by his own kind. He sat there a long time, watching as the sun sank gradually behind the western hills, watching as the flag came down. After retreat he rose and moved slowly inside.

An orderly brought his supper and he ate

without any appetite, his thoughts on Mary Thorne. When they had finally reached the fort, everything seemed so perfect, so uncomplicated, but now the whole thing was at an end.

He had no intention of remaining to stand trial. He had determined that when Mary first told him of the major's plans. He would get away tonight, and he would have to go without telling Mary— without even kissing her again. He thought of her as he had seen her on the trail, as she had looked bathing in the spring, as she had lain, warm and demanding, and he was filled with a physical longing that was harder to bear than the pain of his wounds.

He finished his meal and, without lighting the lamp, moved across the room. It had occurred to no one to disarm him. It apparently had not entered anyone's head that a man who'd had the good fortune to escape from the Apaches once would ever take a chance of trying to cross that country alone again.

The doctor had cleaned his six-gun and it hung in the belt from a peg in the wall. The Winchester stood in the corner. Andy checked them, smiling faintly to himself. He lay down on the bed and pulled the blanket over him. When the doctor came for his last evening call, he pretended to be asleep, and the doctor did not disturb him.

XIX

The rear wall of the doctor's adobe backed flush against the rear wall of the fort. In fact, most of the quarters buildings also served as a part of the fort's light defenses.

It was no trick for Andy to strap on his gun belt, catch up the Winchester, and slip around the corner of the building until he could find a toe hold and thus lift himself to the flat roof. A moment later he dropped lightly beyond the wall, stealing silently across the cleared ground, skirting the huddle of friendly Apache wickiups below the fort where the tame Indians rested uneasily under the watchful eyes of the military.

Beyond and to one side stood the dwellings of the civilian scouts, most of whom had Mexican wives. Then there was the trader's store and the Indian agency.

Andy moved toward the store. It was his intention to steal a horse if possible, but, before he reached the dark building, he passed a small fire and recognized the men around it—three members of his brother's crew. These men were the men who had come in with Gordon, staying here apparently, not guarded, waiting until they could join a detail of troops heading toward Tucson.

He hesitated, watching them from the darkness. None of them had been friends, yet none had belonged to the faction that had lined up behind Gordon. They should, he thought, feel no personal resentment against him. He crept forward until he was within ten feet of the fire, and whistled softly. They straightened, and he spoke in a normal tone. "Don't show surprise. There might be an officer watching. It's Andy Drake. Can you get me a horse and a water bottle?"

A man named Petrie turned, long and lank and usually taciturn. "Why?"

"The major is sending me to Tucson to stand trial for Wakeman's death."

Petrie held his peace. "So we heard. They questioned us all today." He was silent a moment, considering. Then he said: "Go down to the creek bed, a mile below the store, and wait. I'll do what I can. If you hear me whistle three times, show yourself."

Andy faded into darkness. Petrie waited five minutes before he moved unobtrusively away from the fire. Half an hour later Andy heard Petrie's whistle and moved out of the wash to meet him.

The horse was strong and rested. There was a blanket behind the saddle, a water bottle, and a roll of food.

"Head for the border," Petrie told Andy in a low voice. "Keep east of Tucson. Make for Carrizal.

When you get there, ask for Martínez at the first ranch below town. Tell him I sent you."

Andy reached down from the saddle. "Thanks."

"None needed," said Petrie. "I didn't stand with your brother against Gordon, and it makes me feel rotten. *Pasa con Dios.*"

Andy raised his hand, swung the horse, and drove it south along the valley trail. For an hour he held it at a gallop, then he slowed and stopped, getting down to rub the blowing animal with handfuls of dry grass. After the horse had rested, he led it out along the trail, walking. It was no part of his plan to ride the horse into the ground, but he had covered less than two miles when the drum of the hoofs on the hard ground behind him reached his ears.

For an instant he panicked, almost swinging into the saddle and riding away. Then he realized that the sound was made by a single rider. He pulled the rifle from the boot and stood listening. From where he stood a quarter of a mile of the trail was fairly visible in the thin moonlight. He raised the rifle as the rider swept around the curve, and then suddenly lowered it. The rider was Mary Thorne.

She came up to him, fast, and swung down, her horse blowing as she almost jumped into his waiting arms.

"Andy, oh, Andy. You were running out without me."

He held her tensely. "But what are you doing here?"

She kissed him before she said: "I'm going with you."

"But how did you know I was gone?"

"The doctor discovered it. You weren't in bed and your guns were gone. He came and told me, but he didn't tell the major. I don't think he agreed with what the major was doing."

Andy stroked her hair.

"So I went to the crew members for help. I'd talked to them before . . . and this time Petrie told me you were heading for Carrizal. He got me a horse."

"Look," he said, "I love you. I want you more than I've ever wanted anything in my whole life, but I can't take you with me. I've got two hundred miles to cover, country worse than anything we've seen, and foreign. I have no idea what I'll run into, no place to take you, nothing. Use your head, Bantam. By morning the soldiers will be hunting for me."

"I am using my head," she said. "You're the only thing I want. No matter where you go I want to be there."

"But your ranch . . . your father . . . your . . ."

"Hush," she said. "In every woman's life there comes a time when she has to make her choice. I've made mine and I'm not turning back. Come on, Andy, we're wasting time."

"But . . ."

She kissed him. "No buts. Do I have to beg you to take me? Do I have to humble myself?"

"No," he said. "Of course not."

"Then get on that horse, you big ox. They're liable to miss you any time now, and it's going to be a new experience, running away from the cavalry. We'll need all the lead we can get."

She scrambled onto her horse. He grinned in the darkness and rode out with her, for better or worse, and for keeps.

About the Author

Todhunter Ballard was born in Cleveland, Ohio. He was graduated with a bachelor's degree from Wilmington College in Ohio, having majored in mechanical engineering. His early years were spent working as an engineer before he began writing fiction for the magazine market. As W. T. Ballard he was one of the regular contributors to *The Black Mask* magazine along with Dashiell Hammett and Erle Stanley Gardner. Although Ballard published his first Western story in *Cowboy Stories* in 1936, the same year he married Phoebe Dwiggins, it wasn't until *Two-Edged Vengeance* (1951) that he produced his first Western novel. Ballard later claimed that Phoebe, following their marriage, had co-written most of his fiction with him and perhaps this explains, in part, his memorable female characters. Ballard's Golden Age as a Western author came in the 1950s and extended to the early 1970s. *Incident at Sun Mountain* (1952), *West of Quarantine* (1953), and *High Iron* (1953) are among his finest early historical titles, published by Houghton Mifflin. After numerous traditional Westerns for various publishers, Ballard returned to the historical novel in *Gold in California!* (1965) which earned him a Spur Award from the Western Writers of

America. It is a story set during the Gold Rush era of the 'Forty-Niners. However, an even more panoramic view of that same era is to be found in Ballard's *magnum opus*, *The Californian* (1971), with its contrasts between the *Californios* and the emigrant gold-seekers, and the building of a freight line to compete with Wells Fargo. It was in his historical fiction that Ballard made full use of his background in engineering combined with exhaustive historical research. However, these novels are also character-driven, gripping a reader from first page to last with their inherent drama and the spirit of adventure so true of those times.